P9-CRN-819

CONTENTS

Enjoy a sneak preview of Harlequin Everlasting Love™ novels!

This exciting new series offers romance novels that tell the whole story. Because "happily ever after" is just the beginning....

Dancing on Sunday Afternoons
by Linda Cardillo
Available February 2007

As a young woman, Giulia experienced a love that transformed the rest of her life, and, through letters and memories, she shares this story with her granddaughter Cara.

Fall From Grace
by Kristi Gold
Available February 2007

A surgeon and his wife, divorced after being married for more than two decades, discover that memories of their marriage can bring back a love that never really left. Anne was Jack Morgan's first love—and now she's his second chance.

The Depth of Love
by Margot Early
Available March 2007

The deepest feelings last the longest.... Eve Swango and Tommy Baca belong to each other. Always have. Always will. But something within Eve won't allow her to marry Tommy, no matter how often he asks. Each must learn that in the end, love is the only thing that counts.

A Heartbeat Away
by Eleanor Jones
Available March 2007

Daniel Brown promised to love Lucy McTavish forever. But when Daniel is unable to keep his promise, Lucy is left angry, grieving and tries to move on with her life. But when she meets a stranger in a London park, she discovers that Daniel has kept his promise after all—in the most unexpected way.

Look for valuable coupon offers throughout!

ISBN-13: 978-0-373-15097-7
ISBN-10:   0-373-15097-0

Dancing on Sunday Afternoons

Linda Cardillo

On sale February

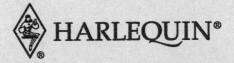

HARLEQUIN®

TORONTO • NEW YORK • LONDON
AMSTERDAM • PARIS • SYDNEY • HAMBURG
STOCKHOLM • ATHENS • TOKYO • MILAN • MADRID
PRAGUE • WARSAW • BUDAPEST • AUCKLAND

PROLOGUE

Two Husbands
Giulia D'Orazio

I had two husbands—Paolo and Salvatore.

Salvatore and I were married for thirty-two years. I still live in the house he bought for us; I still sleep in our bed. All around me are the signs of our life together. My bedroom window looks out over the garden he planted. In the middle of the city, he coaxed tomatoes, peppers, zucchini—even grapes for his wine—out of the ground. On weekends, he used to drive up to his cousin's farm in Waterbury and bring back manure. In the winter, he wrapped the peach tree and the fig tree with rags and black rubber hoses against the cold, his massive, coarse hands gentling those trees as if they were his fragile-skinned babies. My neighbor, Dominic Grazza, does that for me now. My boys have no time for the garden.

In the front of the house, Salvatore planted roses. The roses I take care of myself. They are giant, cream-colored, fragrant. In the afternoons, I like to sit out on the porch with my coffee, protected from the eyes of the neighborhood by that curtain of flowers.

Salvatore died in this house thirty-five years ago. In the last months, he lay on the sofa in the parlor so he could be in the middle of everything. Except for the two oldest boys, all the children were still at home and we ate together every evening. Salvatore could see the dining-room table from the sofa, and he could hear everything that was said. "I'm not dead, yet," he told me. "I want to know what's going on."

When my first grandchild, Cara, was born, we brought her to him, and he held her on his chest, stroking her tiny head. Sometimes they fell asleep together.

Over on the radiator cover in the corner of the parlor is the portrait Salvatore and I had taken on our twenty-fifth anniversary. This brooch I'm wearing today, with the diamonds—I'm wearing it in the photograph also— Salvatore gave it to me that day. Upstairs on my dresser is a jewelry box, filled with necklaces and bracelets and earrings. All from Salvatore.

I am surrounded by the things Salvatore gave me, or did for me. But, God forgive me, as I lie alone now in my bed, it is Paolo I remember.

Paolo left me nothing. Nothing, that is, that my family, especially my sisters, thought had any value. No house. No diamonds. Not even a photograph.

But after he was gone, and I could catch my breath from the pain, I knew that I still had something. In the middle of the night, I sat alone and held them in my hands, reading the words over and over until I heard his voice in my head. I had Paolo's letters.

CHAPTER 1

The Cigar Box
Cara Serafini Dedrick

The phone call didn't come at two in the morning, but it might as well have. I was on my way out the door of my office at four, hoping to catch an early train out of Penn Station and make it home to New Jersey for an early start to my vacation. I run a catering company in Manhattan called Artichoke and in the last weeks of August my clients have retreated to their summer homes, giving me and my staff a breather before fall. Celeste, my secretary, waved to get my attention, receiver nestled between her ear and her capable shoulder.

"It's your mother."

"Tell her I'll call when I get home—got to make the 4:25."

"She says it can't wait. A family emergency."

My body stiffened and I could feel the color drain from my face. My mother was not the kind of woman who called with reports of every hospitalization or divorce or out-of-wedlock pregnancy in our large extended family. With eighteen aunts and uncles and twenty-nine first cousins, plus both grandmothers, there was ample opportunity for a family emergency. But I trusted my mother's sense of what was urgent and what was merely news, and knew she wouldn't insist on talking to me now if it wasn't someone close. Had my father gone into diabetic shock? Was my brother in a car accident?

I turned back to my desk and picked up the phone. "Mom?"

"Cara, thank God you're still there! It's Nana."

My father's mother, Giulia, was a robust woman in her nineties who ran circles around most of us. Three weeks before, against the wishes of all eight of her children, she'd flown to Italy to be at the bedside of her dying older sister. Zia Letitia—we used the Italian form to refer to the aunts of my grandmother's generation—Zia Letitia had graciously managed to wait until Nana arrived before taking her last breath. After she died, Nana had assumed the task of arranging her funeral and organizing her financial affairs. Zia Letitia had been a widow and her only son had died many years before, so there was no one left in the family to wrap up the loose ends of her long life except for Nana. As far as I knew, those tasks were almost finished and she was expected back early the next week.

"What's happened?" I couldn't imagine what could have disrupted my grandmother's determined and vigorous grasp on life.

"She fell last night. It was in Zia Letitia's house. She was alone, and no one found her until this morning. Emma, the woman who looked after Zia Letitia, called to let us know."

"Oh, my God! Is she all right? Where is she now?"

"They got her to a hospital in Avellino, but apparently she's broken her hip. She needs surgery. We thought we could fly her home, but the doctors there said it was too dangerous—the risk of an embolism's too high. Which is why I'm calling you." So it was more than just to inform me of my grandmother's accident.

"What do you mean?"

"We don't want her to go through this alone. It was one thing for her to go off by herself to hold her sister's hand, but now it's simply out of the question. I'd go, but with Daddy needing dialysis every three days, there's no way I can leave him. Nobody else in the family has ever been to Italy— I don't think they even have passports.

"Honey, you've lived in Italy, you speak Italian, and she'd listen to you sooner than one of her children, anyway. I need you to say *yes* about this, especially for Daddy's sake. He's angry with her for going in the first place, angry with himself for letting her go, and now he's feeling helpless— although he won't admit it—because he can't go and rescue his mother. Will you do this, Cara?"

"Do you realize what you're asking me to do?" I groaned. I thought of the two weeks left of summer that I'd planned on spending with my kids. A week at the shore, then a week getting ready for school.

"If you're worried about the kids, I can look after them for a few days, and Paul and Jeannie offered to take them to her mother's house at the lake. There really is no one else who can do this, Cara. I know you think of Nana as formidable and indestructible, but she's in a precarious state."

I listened in silence, watching the minutes pass on the clock on my desk. I'd already missed any chance of making my train. I was both dismayed at my grandmother's situation and frustrated that the competence and independence I had developed in my life apart from my family were now the very things pulling me back. I did not want to go. But I knew I would. I fought the resentment that I was the one my mother had turned to—me, with a very full plate of full-time job and four children—when she could have asked my sister or my cousin, both younger, freer, teachers with summers off and no children. But I was also proud that she'd called on me, knowing she was right when she said I was the only one who could do this.

"I'll need to talk to Andrew and sort everything out with the kids. I'll ask Celeste to book me on a flight to Rome tomorrow and I'll take the train from there to Avellino. Do you have some contact information for me—the hospital, Emma?"

I heard my mother exhale in relief.

"Thank you, honey. I knew I could count on you. I've got all the numbers right here. Let me read them off to you."

I spent the next half hour writing down the information provided by my mother, phoning my husband and giving Celeste the task of getting me to Italy within the next forty-eight hours. I finally collapsed in a seat in the second-to-last car on the 5:43 to Princeton, scribbling lists to myself and trying to remember a language I had not spoken regularly in seventeen years.

The next afternoon, with my husband and children heading off to Beach Haven, my bag packed and my passport in my purse, I drove up to my parents' house in Mount Vernon, just outside New York City. When my mother had called Giulia that morning to tell her I was coming, Giulia had dictated a list for me—things to do, things to bring. I picked up the list and the key to Giulia's house from my parents and said my goodbyes, recognizing the gratitude in my father's eyes despite his gruff warnings about watching out for both my grandmother and myself.

I left my parents' neighborhood of manicured lawns and stately colonials and drove south to the neighborhood my grandmother had lived in since she'd arrived in America. I climbed the steep steps to Giulia's front porch, past the rose garden her husband Salvatore—my father's stepfather—had planted for her in the middle years of their marriage, well before I was born. With Giulia in Italy for the last three weeks, many of the blooms were long past their peak. Had Giulia been here, I know she would've trimmed the flopping, untidy heads.

I let myself in the front door, but not before glancing up and down this so-familiar street. To my right, a row of pale stucco houses, many of which Giulia owned. To my left, the beginnings of commerce—the butcher, the barber, Skippy's Bar & Grill—and on the corner, Our Lady of Victory elementary school. I remembered how one frigid November morning, when I was in kindergarten, I had dutifully exited in a silent, straight line as we'd been trained by the nuns to do when the fire alarm sounded. I'd been careful to line up along the side of the building, trying to keep still in the cold. It had been at that moment that Giulia had emerged from Lauricella's grocery store across the street and observed the shivering children and the sisters bundled in their black shawls.

"Where is your coat? How could that nun let you outside in this weather without your coat?" Giulia stood on the sidewalk and scolded me from across the street.

She was making a spectacle and I was mortified. The only modestly saving grace was that she was speaking in Italian, but her gesturing and agitation were clearly understood by the nuns and my classmates.

"Go back inside this minute and get your coat!"

I wanted to explain to her that this was a fire drill, but was afraid to speak, afraid to break the rules so dramatically presented to us by Sister Agatha as a matter of life and death. Six hundred children had burned to death at Our Lady of the Angels in Chicago because they hadn't followed the rules.

My grandmother knew none of this. She knew only that her grandchild was shivering and the woman responsible for her was ignoring that.

I had watched in horror as Giulia crossed the street, removing her own coat and ready to wrap it around me, when the bell rang and we began to retrace our steps back into the building.

Now, inside Giulia's house, I adjusted to the dim light of the long front hall. The portrait of the Sacred Heart, his hands spreading his cloak to reveal his throbbing scarlet heart, still hung in its place of honor above the radiator.

The house smelled of ammonia and wax and lemon oil. I was sure Giulia had scrubbed and polished meticulously before she left, leaving the house spotless, reflecting her own sense of order.

My sandaled feet echoed in the silent house as I walked down the hall. Although what I'd come for was upstairs in Giulia's bedroom, I went first to the kitchen.

Check the sink, the freezer, the pilot light on the stove, she had instructed. Make sure the back door is secured. Dominic Grazza, her neighbor who was supposed to be watching the house, wasn't as reliable as she would like.

But all was as it should be. I drew myself a glass of water and sat in the red vinyl chair at the small table tucked into the alcove formed by the chimney wall. The table was only large enough for two. Through an archway was the larger table where supper was served, but at noon, when it had only been my grandmother and me, it was at this small table that we'd eaten together. I attended the morning session of kindergarten and came to her house every school day for lunch and to spend the afternoon. She always had ready a warm bowl of her homemade chicken soup or *pasta e fagioli*.

After lunch, when the dishes were dried and put away, I had remained at the table, my back against the warm wall, and watched and listened as women from the neighborhood came for my grandmother's magic.

We called it the "eyes"—her spells to ward off headaches and stomach cramps; to bring on a late period; to counteract whatever curse had been set upon the suffering soul knocking at my grandmother's back door.

It wasn't just the immigrants who came. My own mother, my aunts, women who worked in banks and offices and got dressed in suits and stockings and high heels every day, made their way to her kitchen. There she'd lay her hands on them and dispel the pain with her incantations. When I was sick, the fever and nausea and loneliness flew from my troubled body into my grandmother's open and welcoming arms.

Later in the afternoon, she always went upstairs to sleep, exhausted and without words.

I would retreat to the living room, knowing it was time to be quiet, and watch "The Mickey Mouse Club" until my father came to pick me up at the end of the day.

My afternoons with Giulia were an arrangement put

in place because my own neighborhood had no Catholic school. Sending me to kindergarten in a public school was not an option in our family, so I spent the first year of my education in Giulia's parish until my family moved uptown. Everyone seemed happy with the solution, especially my mother, home with two younger children and relieved of the burden of getting me to and from school every day.

I finished my water, carefully rinsed and dried my glass and replaced it in the cupboard. My responsibilities in the kitchen were fulfilled, and I walked slowly up the stairs to the back of the house, where Giulia's bedroom overlooked the backyard and the garden. On her dresser were propped more images of saints. In front of them were three small red glass pots holding votive candles. It was the first time I'd been in the house when Giulia wasn't there, and it was a disturbing reminder of her absence that the candles were unlit. I pulled out Giulia's list and began to open drawers, tugging at the wood swollen with August humidity. Her checkbook and accounts ledger were in the top drawer, as expected. I had to hunt for the sweater she thought she'd need now that the evening air in the mountains was beginning to chill with the approach of September. A few more small articles of clothing were easier to find. The last item on the list was identified simply as a "cigar box" that was supposed to be in the bottom drawer under some bed linens. I was expecting another set of the flower-sprigged percale sheets and pillowcases that were on her neatly made bed, but these bed linens were heavy white cotton, elaborately tucked and embroidered with Giulia's large and graceful monogram. I had never seen them on her bed. Small packets of cedar were scattered in the drawer and the pungent smell indicated to me that the drawer had not been opened in a long time. I lifted the linens and found a boxlike shape wrapped in another embroidered cloth. When I unwrapped the cloth, I saw that I had indeed found the cigar box.

It was papered in garish yellow and brown with the portrait of some nineteenth-century barrel-chested tobacco mogul on the cover, and a Spanish label. The box had once held Cuban cigars, but I was sure it wasn't cigars I was bringing to Giulia.

I sat on the floor and carefully lifted the cover. Inside the box were stacks of letters on pale blue notepaper, each stack tied with a thin strand of satin ribbon. I could see that the letters had been written in a flowing hand in Italian and signed *Paolo,* the father my father had been too young to know, the grandfather whose red hair I had inherited.

I closed the box, feeling I'd already gone too far, that I had violated the privacy of a very private woman. Why she would want me to remove these letters from what appeared to be a hiding place and carry them across the Atlantic to her was both perplexing and intriguing. The woman who was asking me to do this was not the woman I knew my grandmother to be—the matriarch of our very large family, who had not only her sons and daughters, but her nieces and nephews, grown men and women in their fifties and sixties, listening to her and deferring to her as if they were still children; the businesswoman who'd asked me to collect her mail as well as her checkbook so she could manage her real-estate investments from her hospital bed; the woman who could be counted on to have a sharp opinion and directive about everything that touched the lives of her children and grandchildren.

Perhaps because I'd been a baby when her husband Salvatore had died and I had only known Giulia as a widow, I could not fathom her ever being in love. I knew, of course, that she'd been married before Salvatore to Paolo Serafini. But that had been long ago, and whatever traces of him remaining in her memory were well hidden. We did not even have a photograph of Paolo.

Giulia had never seemed to have much use for love. She had warned me away from romantic entanglements more than once when I was a teenager.

"Stay away from Joey Costello," she told me one evening as we were shelling peas on her front porch. I was thirteen; Joey lived next door to her. He was a year older, full of the swagger and bravado of the good-looking Italian teenage boy. But he had noticed me and was paying attention to me in ways that I, bookish and reserved, found thrilling.

"He's nothing but trouble. You don't need to be hanging around the likes of him. At the very least, you'll get a reputation, like that sister he has. And at the worst, he'll break your heart as soon as somebody who can sway her hips better than you walks by him. You're too smart, Cara *mia*. Don't waste your time on boys like that."

Later, when I was sixteen and spending a week with her while my parents were away, I developed a crush on a neighbor who lived nearby, one of her tenants. He was married and in his twenties, with two small children. But he did chores for Giulia around the garden and the house, so he was around to talk to as he fixed a faucet or dug up some rosebushes she wanted to transplant. He was cute and funny and attentive and, in the short time I'd been there, it seemed to me he was finding quite a few things to do for Giulia. When his wife went to visit her mother with the kids, I suggested to my grandmother that we invite him to Sunday dinner.

"Phil's all alone today. Wouldn't it be nice to ask him to

eat with us?" I was trying to sound like the gracious lady of the manor, bestowing kindness on the hired help, rather than the infatuated teenager I was, looking for any reason to be in his presence. I was nonchalant, mentioning it as an afterthought as she and I cleaned up after breakfast.

Giulia looked me in the eye, put her hands on her hips, and said, "Absolutely not. Don't think I don't know what's going on in your head. He's a married man. He stays in his house and eats what his wife left for him, and you put your daydreams in the garbage where they belong."

And that was that. I spent the day sulking at the lost opportunity and marveling at Giulia's ability to sense even the most subtle vibrations of sexual attraction. She was the watchdog at the gates of my virginity, the impenetrable shield that would keep me from becoming a tramp.

Now I gathered up Giulia's possessions and stowed them in the zippered tote bag I planned to take on board the plane. After a final glance around the room, I shut the door and headed down the stairs and out to my car. I pulled away from the curb and the memories and headed for the airport and Italy.

CHAPTER 2

Journey to the Mezzogiorno

The cacophony of the Naples train station assaulted me as soon as I stepped off the express train from Rome. Announcements of departing trains reverberated across the vaulted space; mothers scolded misbehaving children; whistles shrieked; a group of yellow-shirted boys kicked a soccer ball near the far end of Platform 22.

As I adjusted the strap of my bag, I also adjusted my mental state—from efficient New York manager and organized mother of four—to Italian. It was more than recalling the lyrical language that had surrounded me in Giulia's house. I knew I had to pour myself quickly into the fluid, staccato pace of Campania in August or I would be trampled—by the surging population, the Vespas leaping curbs, the suspicion of strangers and by my own sense of oppression.

I knew this because I'd been here seventeen years before, a bright-eyed high-school art student who'd spent the summer in the rarefied atmosphere of Florence, living in a *cinquecento* villa, painting in the Uffizi on Mondays when it was closed to the hordes of summer tourists, reading Dante and Boccaccio. I had believed that I knew Italy. But then I had come south, to visit Zia Letitia.

I had traveled by rail then as well, through Rome to Naples. A stifling heat had encroached on the overcrowded train as it journeyed farther south, toward an Italy that I didn't recognize. The blue-greens and purples of the Tuscan landscape, warmed by a honeyed light, had given way to an unrelenting sunshine that had seared the earth to an ocher barrenness.

Everything I saw seemed to be the same color—the rough-hewn cliffs, the crumbling houses, the worn faces. When I'd arrived at midday in Naples—sweaty and cranky—I felt myself to be in a foreign country. For the first time in my life, I had felt menaced—by the drivers in minuscule Fiats who ignored traffic signals, by the barricaded expressions of the people massing and knotting around me, by the heat and clamor and stench that had so unraveled the beauty and civility of this once-splendid city. The life of Naples was in the streets—raw, intemperate, flamboyant—and to the eyes of strangers, emotionally closed and hostile.

That day seventeen years ago, I had escaped on the two o'clock bus to Avellina, arriving two hours later in front of a bar named the Arcobaleno. In contrast to the press of humanity in Naples, a melancholy emptiness greeted me here. In the bar, where I bought a Coke and sought a telephone, I was the only woman. Two old men in the corner interrupted their card game to stare openly; the younger men, playing pinball, were more surreptitious but watched just as closely.

I called a phone number given to me by Giulia to make arrangements with a distant relative who could take me to Letitia. But the woman who answered was irritable. She had no time and could not help me. I would have to manage on my own. Take the bus, she barked. Just tell the driver you need to go to Venticano. And she hung up.

Shaken and feeling increasingly alone, I'd found a bus that could take me up the mountain. Later than I'd hoped, the driver cranked the door closed and began the laborious climb out of the valley. He'd brought the bus to a halt in a deserted piazza and thrust his chin at the door to announce my destination. Within seconds I stood alone in the road, facing shuttered houses and an overwhelming sense of abandonment. Why had I even considered making this journey? I had naively traversed half the length of Italy expecting to be welcomed in my ancestral home but instead the doors were locked and no one was willing to acknowledge me as their own.

With only Zia Letitia's name—no address—I had approached a woman darning in the doorway of a nearby house, whose wary eyes had been upon me since I'd descended from the bus.

"I am looking for Signora Letitia Rassina," I had explained, proud of my flawless High Italian, the only thing that stood between me and panic.

"You come from the north." It was a statement, spat out in distrust and contempt, not a question requiring confirmation.

"I studied in Firenze, but I come from America. I am

the granddaughter of Signora Rassina's sister." Unwittingly, I had uttered the magic formula.

The guardedness and suspicion fled from her face. She took me by the arm.

"Come, I'll show you where the signora lives."

As we turned to walk down the hill, I saw faces appearing at suddenly unshuttered windows and heard voices calling out to the woman. Within minutes, nearly thirty people crowded around us, jostling for a glimpse of the Americana as we arrived at Letitia's house.

The house—ancient, once elegant—presented a silent facade to the tumult in the street below. No one responded to our energetic knocks and shouts.

"She must be sleeping. Giorgio, go around and get Emma."

"Emma takes care of your aunt, and she has a key to the house," she explained to me.

A few minutes later, smoothing down what seemed to be a hastily donned black dress, a middle-aged woman had hustled breathlessly after Giorgio with a key ring in her hand.

"No one sent me word from America that someone was coming!" She was both suspicious and injured to have been left out of the preparations for my visit.

Horrified that I'd been allowed by my family to travel alone, she was nevertheless satisfied that I was indeed Giulia's granddaughter. With a shriek of pleasure, she inserted an iron key into the massive arched doorway of the house.

Inside was a musty vestibule, lit by the late-afternoon sun streaming through a window on the rear wall where a stone staircase led to a landing on the second floor. Emma led me up the stairs. Behind us came the rest of the villagers.

Once again, our knocks were met by silence. Emma called out Letitia's name in a loud voice. "She's old. She doesn't hear so well anymore," she murmured to me.

Finally, the door opened and a woman appeared, her face marked by confusion. She stared uncomprehending into my face. I stared back at a woman who could have been my grandmother's twin. Letitia's confusion receded as she listened to me identify myself, ignoring the commotion that surrounded her. Then she reached out and stroked the opal hanging from my ear. It was Giulia's, and she'd given it to me on my sixteenth birthday. I'd been wearing the earrings all summer, and they had become so much a part of me that I'd forgotten their origins.

"Giulia's earrings," she whispered. "You are my blood."

Letitia had pulled me into the apartment, embracing me with the mingled old-woman aromas of garlic and anise and must. She sent Emma down to the shop to purchase ingredients for dinner and told the villagers lining the stairs to go home to their own kitchens. Alone together, we sat with a glass of very strong wine as she hung on every word I brought her of her distant family.

After dinner a group of young women from the village had arrived at the door to take me for the evening *passeggiata*—a walk around the village. Letitia had shooed me away with them. Severia, the young woman who'd been my tour guide, was the schoolteacher in the village. I was stunned when she told me she was only twenty. Like Emma, and nearly every other woman in the village, she was dressed in a severe black dress that extended below her knees. She wore her hair in the style of my mother's generation.

The village was a grid of two or three streets clinging to the side of the mountain. Only the main road from Avellino that continued farther up the mountain was paved. Few of the stone buildings had electricity, and all of them showed the ravages of centuries of wind and earthquake. Dust swirled at our feet as we crossed the meager piazza, shared with a goatherd leading his scraggly flock back to a lean-to for the evening. Severia had pointed out with pride the small school-room where she taught from first through sixth grade. If parents wanted more schooling for their children, they had to send them down the mountain to Avellino.

I had recognized that what I was seeing and the lives that were enclosed here were little different from what Giulia had experienced as a girl. In that instant, I had understood that it might have been my life as well.

"Thank God," I had whispered to myself. "Thank God that my grandmother got out."

The next morning I left, as I had come, on a dusty bus that had stopped when Emma flagged it down. She'd packed me a cloth-wrapped sandwich of bread and pungent cheese, with some tomatoes and figs from the garden behind Letitia's stone house. She had clucked and worried about the long trip ahead of me to Milan and my flight home and had given me stern instructions to speak to no one on the way to Naples.

"Girls alone disappear," she had said.

As the bus pulled away, I had looked out the window. Letitia stood waving from her balcony. She had changed from her morning housecoat to a green silk dress. In her hand was a lace-trimmed handkerchief that she dabbed at her eyes.

I stood now in the rotunda of the Naples *Stazione Centrale,* about to make the same journey. This time, instead of depending on SITA buses to get me up to the mountains, I had reserved a car. But before picking it up, I detoured to the flower shop, hoping to find something that would survive until I reached Avellino. The sales-woman recommended a potted hydrangea and wrapped it extravagantly in layers of purple cellophane and a massive bow, wishing my grandmother *buona sante* as she handed me the gift with a nod of approval.

Armed with a map and directions outlined for me by the clerk at Avis, I located my Fiat in the parking lot, took a deep breath and plunged into the late Sunday afternoon traffic, keeping an eye out for the Autostrada symbol and signs for the A16, the east-west highway that connected Naples with Bari on the Adriatic. About a quarter of the way across the ankle of Italy's boot, I knew I'd leave the highway and head south into the mountains and Avellino.

I was tired and hungry. My jetlag was catching up with me. A part of me longed to stop at the Agip motel on the broad avenue leading toward the entrance ramp of the Autostrada. Its familiar sign, a black, six-legged, fire-breathing mythical creature on a yellow background, beckoned like a McDonald's Golden Arch, promising a cheap, clean room. But Giulia was expecting me at the hospital Sunday evening, and even though there'd be little I could do for her at that time—no surgeon to confer with, only a night nurse on duty—I pushed myself past the fatigue to be at my grandmother's side.

The highway had not existed seventeen years ago, and I was astounded that I was able to cover the hundred kilome-ters to Avellino in under an hour, compared to the nearly three hours it had taken the bus on my last trip. When I exited the highway, a sign welcomed me in four different languages.

When I drove onto the grounds of the hospital of San Giuseppe Moscati, the doctor saint of Naples, it was nearly sunset.

I grabbed the hydrangea and my tote bag from the back-seat and headed into the hospital, moving from the brilliance and shimmer of light and heat that had surrounded me all day into shadowed dimness. Everything in the lobby was in shades of brown, like the sepia tones Renaissance artists used to create the sinopia, the preliminary sketch under a fresco. The highly polished linoleum, the wooden paneling that climbed three-quarters of the way up the whitewashed walls, the tattered seats in the waiting room, even the habit of the Franciscan nun sitting at the reception desk, created an aura of subdued and quiet sanctuary.

She looked up as I approached. When I asked for my grandmother, she jumped up.

"Oh, we've been expecting you! The *signora* was telling everyone that you were coming. Let me call Reverend Mother. She can explain your grandmother's condition before you go up to see her."

Within minutes, Reverend Mother, an energetic and ageless woman and the director of the hospital, swooped into the lobby and kissed me on both cheeks.

"Can I get you some tea, my dear, while we talk about your grandmother? Come, let's go to my office."

I sank into the chair she offered and gratefully accepted the hot cup of tea that she produced within a minute.

On her desk was a file on which I could read my grandmother's name. I was beginning to feel—with some relief, given my fatigue—that Giulia had things under control here, if she had the hospital so well prepared for my arrival.

"Your grandmother is quite a formidable woman, as I'm sure you know. She was very busy the last two days keeping us all informed of your coming. I believe she feels a need to protect and watch out for you. But I must tell you, my dear, she needs *you* to watch over *her,* although she'd be the last to admit it. She's in a weakened state because of the night she spent alone after her fall—we've been replenishing her fluids with an IV, but at her age, even twelve hours of dehydration can be damaging. She was disoriented when she got here. She has recovered her faculties enough to issue edicts and lists, I understand, but I have to caution you that your grandmother has a long road ahead to recover from this fall. In many cases, with patients of this age, we would not even be considering a hip replacement."

I absorbed Reverend Mother's report in silence, gradually comprehending the gravity of my grandmother's condition.

"I hadn't realized how serious this fall was," I murmured. "I naively believed I was asked to be here as a companion to her."

"I'm not trying to overwhelm you and burden you so soon after your arrival, but I felt it was important for you to understand the severity of her injury and to warn you before you see her. She's quite bruised and also very angry with herself for falling. We've also had to increase her morphine dosage because of the pain, so she may begin to drift.

"The surgeon will be in tomorrow morning at eight o'clock and can give you the details about her operation. More than likely he will operate on Tuesday morning."

I nodded, understanding that I would need to be an advocate for my grandmother.

"May I ask you if you've booked a place to stay? If not, I'd like to encourage you to stay here with your grandmother. We can have a cot set up in her room. In my opinion, it would be a blessing for her to have you so close."

I set down my teacup because my hand was shaking. With four children, I'd seen my share of emergency rooms, and my youngest had been hospitalized for four days with pneumonia, so I was no stranger to the emotional fragility caused by illness and the need for a family member to be close at hand. But despite my confidence in Giulia's ability to control even this situation, Reverend Mother had quickly and authoritatively set me straight.

I leaned my elbows on her desk and put my head in my hands. I felt the adrenaline of the last two days seeping out of me and tears of exhaustion and doubt well up. Reverend Mother came around her desk with a handkerchief and put an arm around me.

"Everything Signora D'Orazio has said about you convinces me that your family has sent the right person. Why don't I show you where you can wash your face and then let's go see your grandmother."

Once again, she whisked me down the hall, this time to the ladies' room. When I was ready, we took the elevator up to the orthopedic floor. As we passed open doors, I saw and heard clusters of people gathered around patients' beds, family members taking advantage of the Sunday-evening visiting hours, and was relieved that now Giulia would have someone at her bedside, too, even if what I could offer was simply a voice and a face from home.

Reverend Mother knocked at a partially opened door. "Signora D'Orazio, she's here! Your granddaughter is here!"

I willed a smile to my face and walked into the room.

"Nana," I said. "It's me, Cara."

She turned toward the door and reached out her hand. I was glad Reverend Mother had prepared me, but even so, her bruised and swollen face and the black-and-blue marks on her arm appalled me. She looked as if someone had beaten her, and then I remembered the stone steps in Letitia's house.

I went to her, put the hydrangea on the floor and threw

my arms around her, careful of the IV and reluctant to hold her too tightly for fear of hurting her sore body.

"How good you are to be here!" she whispered.

I sat on the side of her bed and she stroked my hair, by now flying out of its ponytail. She rubbed my bare arms, as if assuring herself that I was truly there.

Reverend Mother left us, letting me know that she was going to order the cot.

Shortly afterward, Giulia's supper tray arrived. When the nun bringing the food saw that I was there, she said she'd call down to the kitchen and have them send something for me. In the meantime, I busied myself with cutting meat and buttering bread for Giulia. She waved me away when I lifted a spoonful of soup to her mouth.

"I didn't break my arm, for God's sake. Just help me sit up a little higher so I don't dribble all over myself."

This was the Giulia I knew, and it was a relief to have her scold me.

By the time we'd both eaten, an aide had delivered a cot, sheets and pillows and made up a bed by Giulia's side. I went down to my car and retrieved my suitcase and then stole a few minutes to peel off the clothes I'd been wearing for two days and take a shower in a bathroom down the hall from Giulia's room that the aide had pointed out to me.

When I rejoined Giulia, she'd had her evening medication, and some of the strain I'd seen in her face was eased. She beamed at me. I was now scrubbed, my hair neatly braided, and wearing fresh clothes.

"Sweetheart, did you bring the things I asked for?"

I patted the tote bag. "It's all in here, Nana. Do you want anything now?"

She wavered, but then threw up her hands as if surrendering to an irresistible need.

"The box. The cigar box. You found it, where I said to look?"

I nodded and dug it out of the bag. "Here it is, Nana."

She took the box and stroked the outside of it, tracing the colorful image of Francisco Fonseca. Then she held the box to her breast, cradling it with her eyes shut. At last, she lifted the cover and stared at the stacks of letters before slipping one out from its ribbon binding. She closed the box and brought the single letter to her lips before unfolding it.

For a few moments I watched as she scanned the lines. I thought she was reading, but then she turned to me in restless exasperation.

"My eyes are no good at night. I can't see the words. Sweetheart, you've done so much, just to come, but do this for me. Read to me. Read me the letter."

She handed me the blue sheet of paper.

I took it hesitantly.

"Are you sure you want me to read this, Nana?"

She looked at me and the letter in my hand, agitation rising in her as she struggled between the absolute sanctity of the message in the letter and the urgency she felt to hear it again.

"I need to hear it tonight, Cara. Go ahead. I trust you."

And so I began to read the words on the page—an elegant, flowing Italian script. At first, my brain attempted to translate silently for myself as I read the Italian out loud, but after a few minutes, I stopped trying to decipher the meaning and simply pronounced the words. I felt as if I were singing a song whose soul and emotion were in the music, not the lyrics.

Dearest Giulia,
Don't forget what I asked you last night—to find five or ten minutes before noon. I have the most important things to communicate to you. If you only knew how much I

*suffered this morning, to go to work without even seeing you
or telling you that I love you.*

*I am crazy with love. I have never loved with so much
devotion. You are the star that shines brightly, a sparkling
beam, and you adorn my poor heart with infinite madness.
Now that I am writing to you, I believe I have you near
me. It seems as if we are talking. How I long to embrace you!*

*I cover your face with my tears, and dry them with my kisses.
Most faithfully,
Paolo*

When I finished, I glanced up. Giulia's eyes were closed
and the agitation that had disturbed her earlier was gone.
I gently removed the cigar box from her lap and put it on
her bedside table. As I reached to turn out the light, she
stirred and touched my wrist.

"Grazie, figlia mia."

I slipped into the cot, the words of my grandfather
Paolo echoing in my head.

★ ★ ★ ★ ★

Read *Dancing on Sunday Afternoons* to discover why
Giulia fell in love with Paolo—and why she *stayed* in
love with him. Linda Cardillo based this moving and
powerful novel on her own grandparents' letters. She was
"fascinated by these two eloquent lovers and inspired to
write a story around this fragment of their history."

Dancing on Sunday Afternoons is on sale January 30 for a
limited time from Harlequin® Everlasting Love™.

Look for savings on the next page.

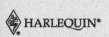

HARLEQUIN®

EVERLASTING LOVE™

Every great love has a story to tell™

Available wherever books are sold, including most bookstores, supermarkets, drugstores and discount stores.

Receive $1.⁰⁰ off

DANCING ON SUNDAY AFTERNOONS
or any other Harlequin® Everlasting Love™ title.

Coupon expires June 30, 2007.
Redeemable at participating
retail outlets in the U.S. only.
Limit one coupon per customer.

113904

5 65373 00076 2   (8100) 0 11390

DSACOUPUS

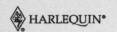
HARLEQUIN®

EVERLASTING LOVE™

Every great love has a story to tell™

Available wherever books are sold, including most bookstores, supermarkets, drugstores and discount stores.

Receive $1.⁰⁰ off

DANCING ON SUNDAY AFTERNOONS or any other Harlequin® Everlasting Love™ title.

Coupon expires June 30, 2007.
Redeemable at participating retail outlets in Canada only.
Limit one coupon per customer.

52607686

Fall from Grace

Kristi Gold

On sale February

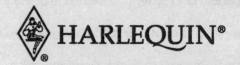

HARLEQUIN®

TORONTO • NEW YORK • LONDON
AMSTERDAM • PARIS • SYDNEY • HAMBURG
STOCKHOLM • ATHENS • TOKYO • MILAN • MADRID
PRAGUE • WARSAW • BUDAPEST • AUCKLAND

Chapter 1

*S*troke.

The word echoed like a canyon shout in Anne Cooper Morgan's addled brain, blocking out the flurry of activity in the Intensive Care corridor, where she had been summoned only moments earlier.

Anne stared blankly at the messenger, Hank Steinberg, Jack's internist and good friend. *Her* one-time good friend, before her and Jack's divorce. "There has to be some mistake, Hank."

He scrubbed a hand over his bearded jaw. "No mistake, Anne."

Not Jack. No way could this have happened to Jack. As far back as Anne could remember, her ex-husband had never caught a cold, even when their daughter, Katie, had brought several viruses home from day care. Jack was obscenely healthy. An avid runner. In all the years Anne had known him, he'd never missed a day of work over health–related problems. He was immortal in everyone's eyes, including his own.

Anne's shock yielded to harsh reality. "How? Why?"

"Aneurysm," Hank said. "He bled out night before last, on New Year's Eve."

"Why didn't someone tell me before now?" She knew the answer to that—because she no longer had a right to know.

"I was out of town, so I didn't learn about it until this morning. I called you as soon as I had the details."

Anne needed more details, although true comprehension still escaped her. "What next?"

"Nan Travers is treating him, which is good, since she's the best neurosurgeon in town. In a couple of hours, she'll determine if he's stable enough for surgery."

"If he survives." Anne posed it as a very real possibility, not a question.

Hank attempted a reassuring smile. "Look, Anne, I have no reason to believe he won't pull through this. He's rela- tively young. Healthy. And because he was here when it happened, he received early intervention." Hank paused briefly before adding, "He's going to make it."

That slight hesitation told Anne more was yet to come. "What are you not telling me, Hank?"

"What he'll be like afterward is my only concern."

Bile rose into Anne's throat, bringing with it the acrid taste of fear. "Paralysis?" The word came out in a croak.

Hank streaked a hand over his nape and studied the blue- and-gray patchwork tiles beneath his feet. "He's exhibiting some on his right side."

"His hand?" She asked the question for Jack as much as she asked for herself. Surgery was Jack's passion. Jack's life. How well she knew that. Their marriage had paid the price for his obsession, and so had their child. But he didn't deserve this. No one deserved this. Even the man who had shattered her heart.

Hank sighed. "The hand's pretty dead right now. The numbness is extensive, especially in his leg. We'll know for sure how bad it might be in the next couple of days, after he's leveled off. If the paralysis doesn't resolve on its own, there's no reason to think he can't recover with extensive rehab. At least, enough to be productive."

"Productive?" Anne released a humorless laugh. "Doing what, Hank? If he can't operate, he'll waste away."

"No, he won't. He'll get better. For Katie. For you."

Anne shook her head. Jack wouldn't get better for her. Maybe for their daughter, but not for her. "He has to do this for himself."

"True. And we have to keep him fighting. We can't lose him over this."

All the well-honed detachment from her former husband couldn't save her from the sudden nausea. Jack was sick. Katie's father. Her one-time husband of seventeen years. Years of abounding happiness and devastating heartache.

She didn't want to feel anything, but she did, and she hated that. "Where is he?"

Hank gestured over his shoulder toward the cubicle. "In eight."

Despite all the latent anger, she had to know he was okay, at least for now. "Can I see him?"

"Sure. He's had some mild arrhythmia, but his pressure's stabilized. Nan's hydrating him with maintenance fluids to prevent cerebral swelling. He's on pain meds, so he's pretty comfortable, but he's still out of it." Hank sent her a comforting smile. "Guess you probably know most of the routine, huh?"

Yes, as a medical professional with years of training, she understood the treatment and the procedures. Right now, though, all that knowledge was useless. She wasn't the R.N. She was the wife—or ex-wife, as was the case. She couldn't exercise solid judgment at a time like this. Not when thinking with her heart, not her head.

"Don't leave anything out, Hank. Assume I know nothing."

"Okay. I'll remember that." He patted her arm. "Right this way."

Anne followed Hank on leaden feet down the hall. Rationally, she knew Jack would simply look like Jack, only asleep. But still she was afraid.

Once they reached the window, Hank stepped to one side and motioned for her to join him. "I'll be back in a few minutes."

Anne moved slowly to the glass and studied the scene. Jack lay on the white-sheeted hospital bed, his six-foot-two frame nearly covering the length of it. With one wayward lock of dark hair falling over his forehead, his mouth slack, he seemed so vulnerable, so unlike the esteemed surgeon who was openly worshiped and silently feared. In that moment she caught a glimpse of the young man she had married—a brilliant doctor, a good friend, an expert lover. Before the drive to be the best had overtaken the tenderness. Before he'd decided that his life's work was more important than his daughter and wife.

Right now Anne wished he would get up and protest, but he remained motionless. The metal bars on the bed had been raised to prevent him from falling. Jack would hate being confined. But it was for his own good, although he would never see it that way.

Anne touched her fingertips to the clear glass, as if she could somehow connect with him. As if she could bring him back to the way he'd been all those years ago, when they were everything to each other. She grieved not only for the Jack whose future was so tenuous, but also for the Jack she had lost to stubborn ambition. The man who had been so easy to love, yet so difficult to understand.

She shook off the memories, though she couldn't shake off the regret, or the groundswell of feelings that she'd tried so hard to disregard over the past two years. She had to keep the painful emotions buried, never to resurrect them again, for the sake of her sanity and her soul.

"He's going to need you, Anne. More than he's ever needed anything in his life."

No. She didn't want to hear this. "Don't do this to me, Hank."

Clasping her shoulders, Hank turned her around to face him. "He's got no one. Just you and Katie. If he's going to survive, he has to have support. He has to have both of you."

Like someone about to tumble over a cliff, she grasped for anything to save her from this fate. "He has a brother."

"Bert's out of the country, Anne. Jack needs friends and family right here to help him recover, and that includes you and Katie."

Anne admitted Hank was right, but her survival instincts were much stronger than logic. This summer she'd planned to cut her hours at the hospital and begin work on her master's degree, bringing her one step closer to realizing her dream— a dream she'd put on hold for the sake of Jack's career. Once she had the degree she could sell the house, with its memories, and start over. She could give Katie a mother who was whole, alive and sure of herself. Jack's need might take all that away. She would suffocate in Jack's need.

Anne tried to stay strong, although she was crumbling inside like week-old pastry. She swiped furiously at the tears that slipped past her attempts to stop them. "Katie's only seven. She wouldn't understand seeing her daddy this way. It would scare her to death."

Hank pinned her with a glare. "Are you intending to keep Katie from him? Are you going to just say, 'To hell with you, Jack. Make it on your own'?" He shrugged. "Of course, you could hire someone to take care of him while he's recovering. Is that what you want, Anne? Strangers tending to him? Do you hate him that much?"

No, she had loved him too much.

Her tears fell in earnest now. She didn't know what to do, what to feel. She only knew she couldn't breathe in this stifling atmosphere. She needed air. She needed to get back to work. She needed to think.

Anne walked away and headed past windows revealing the deluge outside that was no match for the storm of emotions within her. She reached the elevator where she would travel to the labor and delivery floor to resume her shift, a place to forget the prospect of death while welcoming new life. And if that didn't work, she would go home and prepare for her daughter to return from school.

Hank let her go without protest, but she could sense his accusing glare while she waited for the next car to arrive. The doors sighed opened and several people streamed out, family members of loved ones clinging to life. She didn't want to count herself among them, so she brushed past the group, seeking an escape, only to run into another man from her past, hospital administrator Maxwell Crabtree, as always looking polished in his tailor-made blue suit, his thinning sandy hair held in place by a light coat of gel.

Before Anne could hand out a polite greeting and be done

with it, Max took her by the arm and led her away from the elevator. He stopped outside the ICU waiting room, his expression grim. "I've heard about Jack, Anne. Tough break for him."

His tone was less than compassionate—something that didn't surprise Anne in the least. He'd despised her ex-husband for many years. "He'll recover from this, Max," she said, with only minimal conviction.

"I'm sure he will," Max replied. "And I'm sure he'll have plenty of people helping him with that recovery. I only hope you don't get it in your head that you should be one of them."

The exact opposite of what Hank had told Anne a few moments ago. She felt as though she was engaged in a mental tug-of-war of opposite opinions. "This isn't any of your business, Max."

He narrowed his eyes. "You *are* considering it, aren't you?"

Anne could barely think at the moment, much less make any solid plans. "Jack is Katie's father, and Katie needs him. If that means putting aside the past for her sake, then I have no choice."

"Maybe you don't have a choice as far as your daughter's concerned, but you do have a choice when it comes to how involved you're going to be in his life."

Anne tugged her arm from his grasp and backed away. "Again, this isn't your problem. It's mine." A problem that seemed almost insurmountable.

Max slid his hands inside his pockets and leaned against the wall. "I'll still be here for you, Anne, the way I've always been whenever you've needed someone to pick up the pieces after Jack tore you apart. Feel free to call me. Or stop by, day or night, if you want to talk."

An offer she didn't intend to accept this time. "Thanks, but I'll be fine."

Anne rushed back to the elevator and managed to catch a car before the doors closed her out. But she couldn't close out the decision weighing heavily on her heart after Hank's comment had sliced through her mind.

"He's got no one, Anne…. No one but you."

1983

In the country-club ballroom housing Dallas's most prosperous physicians, he stood out like a black diamond against a drift of snow. His stance exuded unmistakable confidence. His unkempt dark hair, faded jeans and sport jacket, sans tie, hinted at the unconventional.

Anne Cooper appreciated anyone who went against the norm in this setting. She detested these New Year's Eve snob-fest soirees. But the stranger across the way had made the obligatory event somewhat bearable. For the past half hour she'd pretended to socialize while covertly watching him, and playing the part of secret admirer suited her fine. Although her mother made an attempt at subtlety, Anne realized Delia Cooper's insistence that her daughter attend the annual shindig had to do with one thing only—introducing Anne to prospects with M.D. behind their names in the hope that she would eventually find one who suited her discriminating tastes.

"His name is Dr. Jack Morgan, Anne."

At the sound of the familiar voice coming from beside her, Anne closed her eyes briefly and muttered a silent oath. She should know by now that her mother qualified as a master mind reader. "I have no idea who you're talking about."

"The man you've been staring at since we arrived."

Anne saw no use in denying her interest. Only mild interest. "Actually, he doesn't look like a typical doctor. Are you sure he is?"

In her usual efficient fashion, delightfully refined Delia sent a wave at the hospital's chief of staff while murmuring through her compulsory smile. "Of course he's a doctor. Everyone here is a doctor. He's a first-year surgical resident. He graduated from medical school with honors—"

"Did you take his résumé at the door, Mother?"

Delia didn't seem the least bit irritated over the question. "Your father's mentioned him a time or two. He claims Jack's going to be a brilliant surgeon. The man also happens to be single, so this is your lucky day."

Lucky? Ha! Maybe if he'd been a tennis pro. For all of her twenty-three years, Anne had been steeped in the sanctity of medicine. Her father was a preeminent surgeon; her mother, a member of every medical auxiliary of acquaintance to God and man and even the inventor of a few; and she herself had become an R.N. She intimately knew the arrogance of physicians, the obsession, the insistence that the lowly folk bow and scrape in their presence. She bowed and scraped for no man.

Before Anne could issue a protest, Delia had her by the hand and was dragging her toward the doctor in question.

Anne stopped dead a few feet prior to the point of no return. "Mother, what are you doing?"

"I'm introducing you. Now, be nice."

"But I don't want—"

"Hush, Anne, and smile."

As much as Anne wanted to run in the opposite direction, as much as she wanted to dive beneath one of the pristine cloth-covered tables, she allowed her mother to lead her forward until she came face to shoulder with the mystery M.D.

Delia patted her blond bob, linked her arm through Anne's and then cleared her throat to garner his attention. "Good evening, Dr. Morgan. I'd like you to meet my daughter, Anne."

Considering his look of surprise, Anne could just imagine what he was thinking—another matchmaking mother foisting her hapless daughter off on a prospective groom. Still, for the sake of civility, she offered a slight smile. "Very nice to meet you, Dr. Morgan."

He gave her hand a brief shake. "It's 'Jack,' and it's nice to finally meet you, too. Dr. Cooper talks about you all the time. I hear you work at the hospital."

The fact that her father had actually mentioned her shocked Anne. Bryce Cooper had never been the demonstrative-daddy type. "I'm a labor and delivery nurse."

"You're at the other end of the building," he said. "That must be why I haven't seen you before. I'm on a general-surgery rotation right now."

Without warning, Delia added, "I'll just leave you two young people to visit," before breezing away with a flip of one manicured hand.

Anne wasn't all that surprised by her mother's abrupt departure. She *was* surprised that Dr. Morgan hadn't made an excuse to do the same. Following a few moments of awkward silence, she said, "Your apparel definitely makes a statement."

He sent her a cynical yet still charming smile. "What? Screw tuxedos?"

Her laughter earned a curious glance from one of the medical matriarchs standing nearby, who was polishing her snobbish air. "I guess you could say that."

"I like what you're wearing. Nothing better than a little black dress."

His tone was suggestive, and that was when Anne decided it would be best to leave, before she began to make a few suggestions of her own. "Again, it was nice to meet you. Think I'll head home."

"Don't go yet," he said. "I could use the company."

"I'm sure you'll find plenty of company as the night wears on." From single women looking for the consummate catch, and she didn't fall into that category.

"I haven't run into anyone here I care to keep company with. Too much bowing and scraping."

Surely he hadn't really said *bowing and scraping*. "Excuse me?"

When a roving waiter passed by, Jack snatched two glasses of champagne from the tray and offered her one. "You know, kissing ass for the sake of appearances. I work forty-eight-hour rotations, and I can think of several things I'd rather be doing in my spare time than sucking up."

So could Anne, even if it meant curling up on the couch in her apartment and ringing in the new year alone. "I know what you mean. I'm only here because my mother asked me to come. I need to get a life." Wonderful. She'd just admitted she didn't have one.

He downed the wine in two gulps, then set the glass on the portable tray behind him. "This is going to sound crazy, but I really want to play miniature golf. There's a place on the interstate a few miles away. Are you interested in a game?"

She tightened her grip on the flute as if it were a life jacket capable of saving her from sinking. "Let me get this straight. We've just met and you want me to play miniature golf with you in the dead of winter while I'm wearing a cocktail dress and three-inch heels."

"It's not that cold."

"It's forty degrees out."

"If you don't own a coat, you can borrow mine."

Obviously he'd mistaken her for a fool. "Of course I own a coat."

"Then what's the problem?" When Anne didn't immediately respond, he added, "We only have to play one round. Of course, if you have other plans for the evening, we can do it some other time."

Faced with a situation that meant destroying her pride if she told the truth, she considered a small lie. Yet for some reason, either a lapse of sanity or unseen cosmic forces, she found herself saying, "Actually, no. I don't have any plans. But we barely know each other."

"What's your favorite color?" he asked.

"Red."

"Red's good. Now it's your turn."

Anne thought a moment. "What's your favorite sport, aside from miniature golf?"

"Baseball."

This might go somewhere after all. "I'm a rabid baseball fan."

"Great. Now, one more question," he said. "Why didn't you go to medical school?"

The question she'd been asked at least a thousand times. "You sound like my father. He's never understood why I didn't want to wield a scalpel and a mammoth ego. The truth is, I prefer the personal connection with patients, not to mention keeping doctors in line. You and I both know doctors are nothing without nurses."

He held out his hands, palms forward. "I guess I've touched on a sorry subject."

"You would be right."

He tried on an apologetic look, and it worked well. "I agree—doctors can't function without nurses. Okay?"

Suddenly she felt a little foolish over her semirant. "Okay."

"Go ahead and ask me something really personal."

Anne grabbed the opportunity to do a little fishing. "How many women have you propositioned tonight?" She watched for signs of discomfort in his demeanor, but found none. Then again, he could be very good at masking guilt.

"I'm taking the Fifth on that," he said.

Which probably meant he'd delivered too many propositions to count. "You don't play fair, do you? And that really makes me wonder if I should join you in that golf game."

"Are you worried I'd beat you?"

Anne's competitive nature planted a swift kick to her common sense. "That never entered my mind because it's not going to happen. I'm good."

"So am I. Better than most, in fact."

She downed the rest of her drink, ready to meet the challenge. After all, it was only a game. Mindless recreation. She could do mindless, even if she didn't do doctors. "Okay, you're on. And you're paying."

"Believe me, Annie, you're definitely worth the price."

She should have been insulted that he'd called her "Annie," a nickname she'd never cared for. She should rescind the offer and get away fast. But sometimes those "shoulds" weren't at all appealing. "Let's just see if you say I'm worth it when I kick your butt, Dr. Morgan."

Anne expected a comeback, but instead Jack studied her

awhile before he said, "Do you want an honest answer to your earlier question?"

"That would be nice." She expected honesty from a man. In fact, she demanded it.

Jack surveyed the room for a moment, as if preparing to tell a secret, before he leaned close to her ear and whispered, "You're the only one."

* * * * *

Can Jack and Anne Morgan recover what they've lost?
Can a broken marriage be mended?
Do you ever get a second chance with your first love?
Read *Fall from Grace* by award-winning author Kristi Gold
to find out. And discover why this book has been called
"a must read and a definite keeper!"

Fall from Grace is on sale January 30 for a limited time from
Harlequin® Everlasting Love™.

Look for savings on the next page.

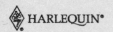
HARLEQUIN®

EVERLASTING LOVE™

Every great love has a story to tell™

Available wherever books are sold, including most bookstores, supermarkets, drugstores and discount stores.

Fall from Grace
Kristi Gold

Receive $1.⁰⁰ off

FALL FROM GRACE
or any other Harlequin®
Everlasting Love™ title.

Coupon expires June 30, 2007.
Redeemable at participating
retail outlets in the U.S. only.
Limit one coupon per customer.

RETAILER: Harlequin Enterprises Limited will pay the face value of this coupon plus 8¢ if submitted by the customer for this specified product only. Any other use constitutes fraud. Coupon is nonassignable. Void if taxed, prohibited or restricted by law. Void if copied. Consumer must pay for any government taxes. Mail to Harlequin Enterprises Ltd., P.O. Box 880478, El Paso, TX 88588-0478, U.S.A. Cash value 1/100¢. Limit one coupon per customer. Valid in the U.S. only.

113912

5 65373 00076 2 (8100) 0 11391

FFGCOUPUS

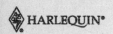

HARLEQUIN®

E V E R L A S T I N G   L O V E™

Every great love has a story to tell™

Available wherever books are sold, including most bookstores, supermarkets, drugstores and discount stores.

Receive $1.⁰⁰ off

FALL FROM GRACE
or any other Harlequin®
Everlasting Love™ title.

Coupon expires June 30, 2007.
Redeemable at participating
retail outlets in Canada only.
Limit one coupon per customer.

CANADIAN RETAILERS: Harlequin Enterprises Limited will pay the face value of this coupon plus 10.25¢ if submitted by the customer for this specified product only. Any other use constitutes fraud. Coupon is nonassignable. Void if taxed, prohibited or restricted by law. Void if copied. Consumer must pay for any government taxes. Nielson Clearing House customers ("NCH") submit coupons and proof of sales to: Harlequin Enterprises Ltd., P.O. Box 3000, Saint John, N.B. E2L 4L3. Non–NCH retailer—for reimbursement submit coupons and proof of sales directly to Harlequin Enterprises Ltd., Retail Marketing Department, 225 Duncan Mill Rd., Don Mills, Ontario M3B 3K9, Canada. Limit one coupon per customer. Valid in Canada only.

52607699

FFGCOUPCAN

The Depth of Love

Margot Early

On sale March

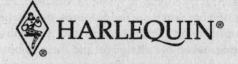

HARLEQUIN®

TORONTO • NEW YORK • LONDON
AMSTERDAM • PARIS • SYDNEY • HAMBURG
STOCKHOLM • ATHENS • TOKYO • MILAN • MADRID
PRAGUE • WARSAW • BUDAPEST • AUCKLAND

CHAPTER 1

Eve
Rancho Ventoso, New Mexico
October 31, 1977
The Beginning

Eve Swango was born on Halloween, which meant birthday parties were sometimes lost in the excitement of the school parade, of Halloween cupcakes and trick-or-treating. And of course, in Viento Constante, Halloween was less of a big deal than Todos Santos, the celebration of All Saints' Day on November first and All Souls' Day on the second, when her classmates and their families visited the graves of loved ones, often leaving cempasúchil, the yellow marigold, bought at the market outside town. Eve minded none of this—it made her feel special in a way she couldn't articulate, to have been born on All Hallows' Eve.

In any case, this year she was ten, and her mother had promised her a slumber party.

Her mother had said she could invite up to six friends, but even after a year and a half in Viento Constante, Eve wasn't sure six girls would come to her house. She was the only Anglo in her grade, and even the Spanish she'd learned from Rosa and Felix, the Swangos' "help"—when her mother wasn't around to know about it—could not make her something other than Anglo.

She'd invited Cecilia Martinez, Maria Ortiz and Patty Romero.

She had dressed as a soccer player for Halloween. Eve had some ambition to be a professional soccer player, not for the fame but because she loved the game and was good at it. Besides, the costume was comfortable, even for the last day of October. She kicked a ball all the way home from school, picking goals between junipers along the dirt roads, nailing boulders, running to dribble the ball back to the road. When she reached her house, she went first to see her horse, Magic, who was of mustang stock and had been gentled by Felix and was now twelve years old. "I'm having a birthday party," she told the horse. She could already smell fry-bread from the kitchen; it would be her afternoon snack.

When she entered the kitchen of the big adobe house, a strange boy sat at the heavy wood table. His hair was so long that at first Eve wasn't sure he *was* a boy. He wore the kind of cheap jeans that never fade and a black T-shirt with an elaborate painting of the Virgin of Guadalupe on the back. He was taller than Eve and older, though not as old as her sister, Cimarron, and Eve suspected he was both Spanish and Native American, which some people were.

Rosa, whose back was to the door, sang, *"Voy a cantarles un corrido muy mentado/Lo que hapasa do allá en la hacienda...."*

Eve loved to listen to Rosa sing. Rosa had taught her many songs, and Eve sang them sometimes when she was out riding Magic.

The boy stared at Eve. His eyes seemed almost black, and his face was fierce, like a hawk's.

Rosa looked around, broke off her song. "There you are. Go wash your face and hands, and you can eat and meet Tommy. Tommy Baca. He's going to live here."

A stranger would come to live with her family? Impossible. "No, he's not," she said and leaned toward the counter to see her birthday cake, which she had only just noticed. It was covered with pink roses. *HAPPY BIRTHDAY, EVE* crossed the white icing in pink froth. Undoubtedly, Eve's mother had told Rosa what to do. Eve would have preferred a cake the way Rosa made it without her mother's input. She had begged for a piñata, too, and Daisy had refused, asking her if she wanted to be like one of her wetback classmates. Eve hadn't known what that word meant, only that it was sufficiently offensive for Felix, who had overheard, to tell Eve's father, in rapid and arrogant Spanish, that his family had been in this valley since the seventeenth century.

But Eve still had no piñata.

Cimarron came into the kitchen and leaned against the doorway, her black hair bouncing around her shoulders like one of Charlie's Angels. Her smile to Eve was fake—part sarcastic, part disgusted. Cimarron was a person to be treated with caution. She went away to school—boarding school—and she was already a model and had been to Europe and had her photo in big magazines. The pictures didn't really look like her, though. She told Eve scary things that Eve's father said were nonsense but that Eve couldn't forget—for instance, that in the *morada,* the Peni-

tente church on their property, *Los Hermanos de Luz* cru-
cified people and next Lent Eve would be chosen to die.
Felix, Cimarron said, was a Penitente, one of the Broth-
erhood of the Light, some kind of Catholics who did all
the scary things in the Bible for real, and he'd already
picked Eve for crucifixion. Now Eve's half sister said,
"Have you seen what Dad brought home?"

Eve's father was a geologist, and he taught at the local
community college, although he used to be a professor at
the university in Santa Fe. He wanted, he said, to be closer
to his family. He brought home fossils and mineral speci-
mens. When he went to Santa Fe as a visiting lecturer or
on other business, he brought back jewelry for Cimarron
and sometimes a doll or a kachina for Eve, who had a col-
lection of these in her room. "What?" Eve asked.

"That."

"You are a very rude girl," Rosa exclaimed. "You get
out of my kitchen until you're ready to act like a lady. They
taught you no manners in Paris?"

"He's our new foster brother, our very own gutter
child."

Rosa turned away and began muttering under her
breath in Spanish, furiously splashing dishwater in the sink.

Eve thought Tommy looked as if he belonged in a
gang. But she wasn't afraid of him. She said, "Can you
ride a horse?"

"Don't like that stuff," he told her.

"You should learn to like some things that are good for
you," Rosa told him. She told Eve, "He is to live with Felix
and me. Felix and I have been visiting him at his orphanage for a few months now, and today your father and Felix
brought him home to live with us."

Eve thought this was interesting. Her mother said Rosa and Felix weren't "able to have children."

"Evie," Cimarron said in a sweet voice that instantly made Eve suspicious, "let's go practice the piano. I have to tell you a secret."

Eve decided to ignore her. Cimarron had already given dark hints of what *Los Hermanos* had planned for *Todos Santos*. Eve didn't want to know. She told Tommy, "I'll let you ride my horse. If you're going to live here, I bet my dad will get you one of your own."

"Eve, come here *now*." Cimarron's voice carried warning.

Eve followed slowly, and Cimarron told her not to play with that boy. "He was sent to live with us because, at his orphanage, he ate someone's dog. Don't let him ride Magic. He might want to eat him next."

Eve recognized that this was one of her sister's scary stories, yet it painted a horrible image she knew would give her bad dreams. What kind of person ate dogs? *You're lying.* She didn't say it because Cimarron would pinch her.

"You should call your friends and tell them not to come. Mother's been having bourbon since two o'clock."

This was not a lie, would not be a lie. Her mother was drunk. Eve knew what drunk was. Her mother would play the piano and sing old songs from musicals and maybe dance. She would talk about how much better her life was before she became pregnant with Cimarron. She discussed things Eve didn't wholly understand.

"So what?" Eve said. Her mother was drunk. Eve didn't like her mother drunk, but she still intended to have a slumber party.

Heels sounded on the wood floor, and Daisy Lee Swango appeared. She wore a full-skirted dress with short cap sleeves. Cimarron and their mother were built alike. Tall, with curves. Eve thought her mother looked pretty. She had her black hair up in what Daisy called a French twist, and she wore glittery earrings shaped like tears.

"Eve, darling, it's getting late. You need to hurry and put on your dress before your friends come."

Eve hated to wear dresses. She wore them on Sundays and on holy days and detested every minute of it. Her mother had grown up in Virginia, and Cimarron said that was why she liked dresses so much. Eve also knew it was why her mother talked with an accent.

"We're all wearing our Halloween costumes," she said, "because we're going trick-or-treating. Dad promised to take us."

"Oh." Her mother's eyes rounded in exaggerated surprise. All her expressions were bigger than other people's. "No one told me."

Eve herself had mentioned it to her mother *yet again* only the night before. She hadn't said anything about it that morning because she never saw her mother before school. If her father was out of town, it was always Rosa who woke her, made sure she had her lunch and everything she needed. This morning, it had been Rosa.

"Well, you should put on a nice dress before you go trick-or-treating. You can change into your costume later. Did you have soccer practice today?" she asked vaguely.

"This *is* my costume, and I want to wear it for my party. Who's that boy?"

"An orphan Rosa and Felix have agreed to take in."

Cimarron had been right about the orphan part; maybe she'd been right about the reason Tommy was no longer at the orphanage. But she *couldn't* be. Rosa and Felix lived in the little adobe house Daisy called "the caretaker's cottage." So Tommy Baca would be living in that house, not in the big house where Eve lived with her sister and parents.

Her mother pirouetted gracefully and sang the opening lines to "Oh, What a Beautiful Morning" as she made her way to the sideboard. She frowned for a moment, as though looking for something she'd lost, then shrugged and took down a clean glass.

Eve glanced at the grandfather clock against the wall. Her friends would be arriving soon.

Cimarron gave her a what–did–I–tell–you? look. Eve ignored her, not seeing any reason her slumber party should be canceled.

An hour and a half later, she began to see.

Cecilia, as a white rabbit, Maria as a ballerina and Patty as a nurse sat politely on the couch in the living room while Daisy held forth. Daisy poured herself another glass of bourbon from a bottle she had now decided to keep close at hand. She was trying to feed film into an eight-millimeter projector, and the first titter escaped Cecilia, who whispered to Maria in Spanish.

As if Eve didn't know the meaning of *ebria*.

"Well—" With a shrug, Daisy gave up on the film. "I'll *tell* you about it. The casting couch was not a thing of the past then, nor is it today, and I don't mind saying I paid *all* my dues. Why pretend otherwise?"

None of them had the slightest idea what she meant.

"I auditioned with the best…." Her eyes misted over and a tear ran down one cheek.

Mother! Eve objected silently. *Why do you have to do this to me?* Her father had office hours at the college and wouldn't be home until six-thirty, just in time to take them trick-or-treating. There was no Pin-the-Tail-on-the-Donkey, no Musical Chairs.

Eve turned to the three girls on the couch. "Let's go outside." As she jumped up, she spotted the figure slouched in the doorway and wondered how long he'd been there.

But he turned swiftly, and a moment later, she heard him speaking Spanish to Rosa in the kitchen, though too fast for Eve to understand.

Rosa protested no, that Señora Swango had said no.

But the boy's voice took on a charming, fond, wheedling tone that caught Eve's ear at once. Sweet and affectionate, generous and loving. Another side to a shadow of anger she'd sensed in him from the first. He said he didn't need whatever it was. Again, that word for drunkenness.

"Tomasito," Rosa said kindly, and Eve imagined her cuffing the boy lightly on the ear. Clearly, Rosa liked him.

Looking back to make sure the other girls followed, Eve started out of the room.

"No!" her mother insisted. "I know what mothers do. I'll teach you dance steps. Don't you want to learn to dance?" she implored of the white rabbit.

Cecilia's face crumpled in fear.

Eve said firmly, "No, Mother, we're going *outside*.". She grabbed Maria's arm to lead her out of the room, and the other two girls hurried after them. "Let's go pet Magic," she said as she passed through the kitchen, now empty.

But when they stepped onto the flagstone threshold, the orphan called Tommy blocked the way. He stood on a rickety wooden extension ladder, suspending a piñata, an enormous elephant, from a stout oak limb near the doorway. Felix crossed the patio bearing a heavy rake or shovel handle and a rag for a blindfold.

The four girls began jumping up and down, and soon they were being blindfolded, one after the other, and turned three times. Each swung at the piñata while the others shouted,

"¡Dale! ¡Dale!" *Hit it! Hit it!* as Tommy pulled the rope to draw the candy-filled papier-mâché elephant up and down.

Eve went last and felt the bat connect hard with the piñata, and the girls cried out.

As she removed the blindfold, Rosa whispered to her, "You must thank Tommy. It was his, for his birthday in a week. Your father bought it for him on the way here from the orphanage."

Eve straightened and looked curiously at Tommy. She brought him the bat. *"Gracias,"* she said. "You have a turn. You can break it."

"All of you," he said, "go again, and then I will. *Tio* Felix can pull the rope."

Eve stared into his eyes for a moment, the person who had done such a fine thing. The piñata might help her friends forget Daisy Lee Swango's trying to show them her bit parts in 1960s B-movies, which was what Cimarron said their mother had done a long time ago and which made no sense to Eve. Surely it was impressive to be in a movie at all, and her mother was a very accomplished dancer. A *B* wasn't a bad grade, Eve knew, although it wasn't as good as an *A*.

But she remembered Daisy's tears and her incomprehensible monologue and she vowed, neither for the first nor the last, never to be like her mother. Not in any way at all.

Then, who was she supposed to be like? She could be like her father—except that she wasn't a man.

Tommy
The next school day

Rosa and Felix have kept me with them during *Todos Santos.* When they came to the orphanage the first time and wanted to meet me, I was sure it was for nothing good.

Now, it's sixth months later, and I live with them and these other people and go to school in Viento Constante, and everyone's waiting for me to screw up.

One day at school. I haven't screwed up yet.

After school, the girl called Eve says, "Tommy, come outside."

She's not a bad kind of girl, and I feel sorry for her because her mother's a drunk. That's why I gave her the piñata on her birthday. Now it's Monday, and I follow her outside the house, the old-style hacienda, one of the rich houses of old New Mexico. I don't belong here, but she doesn't either, even though her parents own this place, the Rancho Ventoso.

"Magic is over here," she says, skipping. She's a very *little* girl. Her sister, the junior model, is full of herself, but this one's okay, just a little kid. "Do you know how to ride horses?" she asks. "It's easy. I can change the stirrups for you and everything, and Magic is old and quite gentle."

"I don't want to ride him," I say. I've ridden horses—on special occasions, field trips for some of the orphans. Felix has said I'll "learn to ride" here, on the Swangos' ranch, because he can teach me about horses. *But horses,* Felix said, *will teach you more themselves.*

Eve's horse looks old and tired. She has brought him a piece of apple. "Pet his nose," she tells me. "And he likes you to blow on his nose like this." She demonstrates.

I hang back.

The little girl, Eve, leaves her horse. "Have you met the dogs?" She seems worried. "They're Felix's," she adds, as though that's supposed to make some difference to me. "Do you play soccer?"

"Like, on a team?"

She nods.

"No."

Her eyes are so dark brown they're almost black. She says, "Do you have brothers or sisters?"

"No."

"Where did you used to live?"

It must be nice to be a little girl like that who isn't afraid of asking whatever she wants to know. "In an orphanage. A Catholic boys' home."

"Do you have parents? Or are they dead?"

"I don't know."

She looks so sad I think maybe she feels it just as though she's the one who doesn't know about her parents.

I tell her, "Someone left me outside the orphanage the night I was born. I don't know who my parents were. Felix and Rosa say they're going to be my parents now."

"I'll be your sister!" she offers at once.

This almost makes me laugh.

"I've never had a brother, and I don't always like my sister."

Now, that's good judgment, in my opinion.

I don't tell her she can be my sister. It's not going to last, staying at this place. I've seen other kids leave the orphanage and then come back when it "doesn't work out." Nothing lasts. I told Felix that, and Felix said, *Except God.* I wanted to say I don't believe in God. Instead, I played along with Rosa and Felix's way of looking at things.

For now, I'm playing, that is.

I tell Eve, "I'll be your friend."

"Then, come on. I'll teach you how to play soccer." She runs.

She runs all the time.

Tommy
Friday before Holy Week, 1980

Eve's father lies in his casket in the living room, which is full of flowers. Daisy is drunk.

★ ★ ★

Eve has that look on her face that says she can't stand her mother. But if she walks away now, Daisy will accuse *her* of abandonment.

I say, "Want to go outside?"

"Yes."

"You young people," Daisy tells us, "just want to be together. You only think of each other, no one else. And Eve, you're going to get into trouble soon. You don't know what's what."

I understand what Daisy means, but I'm not sure Eve does. Eve has braces and acne, and it's a bit hard to imagine that Daisy is right.

Eve says, "Come on, Tommy," and marches toward the kitchen, toward escape.

Outside, we walk to the cave, the Rancho Ventoso's own cave that's just one room with a sandy floor.

I offer Eve a cigarette, and she takes it. I smoke Marlboros. She prefers Virginia Slims, which Cimarron buys her during her lifetime's three seconds of being nice. I light our cigarettes and we smoke as we walk to the cave.

"I can't stand it," she says. "I can't stand it that he's gone, Tommy."

And she cries.

Eve's crying is worse than anyone else's. I'd never seen her cry until her dad died in the cave.

I don't know what to do. She loved her father. I loved him, too. Felix and Rosa are good. But besides Eve, Peter was the only sane Swango. Now, Eve's on her own. Except for me...

"I can't stand it," she repeats, sobbing.

I put my arm around her because she's like my little sister. I turn her toward me and hug her, both of us holding our cigarettes clear. It feels a little strange, a little like hugging other girls.

Not sisters.

I let go, and she wipes her eyes and her face with her shirt, before she's ready to walk on.

"She didn't even appreciate him," she says. "My mom. She complains all the time about how he brought her to New Mexico, as though…as though he imprisoned her by marrying her. Cimarron's father never married Daisy. You know what *that* means."

I think about what this might mean. "What?"

"Well, he didn't love her. Obviously."

I connect those thoughts. To love a woman is to marry her. Is this true? Someday I will marry someone and have lots of kids. If that happens, it'll feel as if I know my lineage back to the fifteenth century. I'll be a patriarch, living on land that's been in my family's hands since before New Mexico was New Mexico. But that's not true. I don't know where I came from and never will. I was left at the orphanage as a newborn, probably hours after I was born. No note. No way to know where I came from. Baca was Father Frank's last name. He gave it to me so I'd have one.

We reach the cave, and the wind is blasting the way it always does there. We stand in it, finishing our cigarettes. Eve tells me, "She's drunk *all* the time. My father took care of her. Now *I'm* going to have to. Someone has to."

This is true. "Maybe she'll marry some other guy. She's beautiful." I wish I didn't say that because it's weird. But everyone knows Eve's mom is beautiful and Cimarron is even more beautiful—strictly on the outside, of course.

Eve is not good-looking that way.

Eve is watching me strangely, and I *feel* strange. Daisy is always saying what a handsome young man I am, which I wish she wouldn't. Rosa says it, too, but the way she says it is different. Rosa speaks the way a mother or a *tia* should, and she always says if only I'd learn to *act* decently…

With Daisy, it's different. Daisy expects people to think she's beautiful and guys to want her. Everybody, from me to the oldest man in Viento Constante. This is kind of bizarre, if you ask me.

"No one's going to marry her," Eve says. "She's a drunk. Everyone in New Mexico knows it."

Never get on Eve's bad side. She can dish it out.

We stub out our cigarettes and go down into the cave with no lights. We know this tiny room. It's just a little cave, but I like how you have to go *down* into it, and when you're down you can hear the wind sing.

When we're standing in the room, we play the hand game. The point of the hand game is to tap the other person's hands, sometimes one at a time, sometimes both, and to challenge the other person to touch yours and to know where all the hands are even though we can't see them. It's hard to explain, but I'm great at the hand game, and Eve's pretty good, too.

Finally, we sit down. I can't see her, but I'm sure she sat down in her skirt to annoy Daisy. Eve is a tomboy to keep herself from being like Daisy and Cimarron.

"I am never getting married," she tells me, which I could well imagine to be true. She's not that cute. "I'm never going to be like *her*. She's not even a grown-up. Do you know what I mean? She needs someone to take care of her, and she's always going to be that way."

"Men take care of women."

I hear her breath. Now she's mad.

"No one's going to take care of *me*. Because if people take care of you, they also want to tell you what to do."

Why do I feel sorry for her? She doesn't trust anyone

to take care of her—well, she trusted her dad. But she acts like she's going to have to do everything herself from now on. *Don't make things so hard on yourself, Eve.*

I say, "You'd let me tell you what to do."

"Oh, try it."

That makes me laugh. But I can't think of a dare she won't take—although accepting a dare is not the same as letting yourself be told what to do.

"I'll always be here, Eve. I promise."

Her voice comes back in the dark. "Thanks." She sounds sulky but also comforted, and I think for a second that I'm going to know Eve for the rest of my life.

★ ★ ★ ★ ★

Eve Swango and Tommy Baca—they love each other but life keeps getting in the way. Is their love deep enough to keep them together through the years?
Read *The Depth of Love* to find out.
You'll also learn why *New York Times* bestselling author Debbie Macomber says Margot Early "writes with warmth, wit and emotional depth."

The Depth of Love is on sale February 27 for a limited time from Harlequin® Everlasting Love™.

Look for savings on the next page.

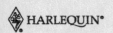

HARLEQUIN®

EVERLASTING LOVE™

Every great love has a story to tell™

Available wherever books are sold, including most bookstores, supermarkets, drugstores and discount stores.

Receive $1.⁰⁰ off
THE DEPTH OF LOVE
or any other Harlequin®
Everlasting Love™ title.

Coupon expires June 30, 2007.
Redeemable at participating
retail outlets in the U.S. only.
Limit one coupon per customer.

RETAILER: Harlequin Enterprises Limited will pay the face value of this coupon plus 8¢ if submitted by the customer for this specified product only. Any other use constitutes fraud. Coupon is nonassignable. Void if taxed, prohibited or restricted by law. Void if copied. Consumer must pay for any government taxes. Mail to Harlequin Enterprises Ltd., P.O. Box 880478, El Paso, TX 88588-0478, U.S.A. Cash value 1/100¢. Limit one coupon per customer. Valid in the U.S. only.

113920

5 65373 00076 2   (8100)0 11392

DOLCOUPUS

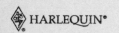

HARLEQUIN®

E V E R L A S T I N G   L O V E™

Every great love has a story to tell™

Available wherever books are sold, including most bookstores, supermarkets, drugstores and discount stores.

Receive $1.⁰⁰ off
THE DEPTH OF LOVE
or any other Harlequin®
Everlasting Love™ title.

Coupon expires June 30, 2007.
Redeemable at participating
retail outlets in Canada only.
Limit one coupon per customer.

CANADIAN RETAILERS: Harlequin Enterprises Limited will pay the face value of this coupon plus 10.25¢ if submitted by the customer for this specified product only. Any other use constitutes fraud. Coupon is nonassignable. Void if taxed, prohibited or restricted by law. Void if copied. Consumer must pay for any government taxes. Nielson Clearing House customers ("NCH") submit coupons and proof of sales to: Harlequin Enterprises Ltd., P.O. Box 3000, Saint John, N.B. E2L 4L3. Non–NCH retailer—for reimbursement submit coupons and proof of sales directly to Harlequin Enterprises Ltd., Retail Marketing Department, 225 Duncan Mill Rd., Don Mills, Ontario M3B 3K9, Canada. Limit one coupon per customer. Valid in Canada only.

52607703

DOLCOUPCAN

A Heartbeat Away

Eleanor Jones

On sale March

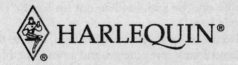

HARLEQUIN®

TORONTO • NEW YORK • LONDON
AMSTERDAM • PARIS • SYDNEY • HAMBURG
STOCKHOLM • ATHENS • TOKYO • MILAN • MADRID
PRAGUE • WARSAW • BUDAPEST • AUCKLAND

There was a place halfway up the far meadow where the ground leveled off, close to where the stream tinkled over the rocks in a mini waterfall. A sprinkling of buttercups made a bright yellow pattern against the vivid green of the grass. I looked around, entranced, and as my eyes fell upon the sea of blue beneath the trees, their fragrance hit me.

"Bluebells," I cried, breathing in their glorious scent.

"Come on," he said, holding out his hand. "Let's have our picnic here."

He led me to a place beneath the trees, next to the silver stream, and I sank onto the ground among the bluebells.

"This—" I announced with a sweeping hand "—is magic."

Daniel grinned and began emptying the rucksack onto the ground.

"And so is this!" he exclaimed. "Mother has done us proud today. She must have known it was special."

Special? A prickle ran down my neck and my heart started to beat in my ears. Was today really special?

"Dig in," he ordered. I turned my attention to the feast that he had spread out on the ground. Thick, home-cooked ham sandwiches, sausage rolls fresh from the oven and a huge variety of mouthwatering tasty scones and pastries. Hunger pangs took over, and I closed my eyes and bit into soft homemade bread.

When we were finally done, I lay back against the bluebells with a groan, clutching my stomach.

Daniel laughed. "Your eyes are bigger than your stomach," he told me.

I leaned across to deliver a punch to his arm, but he rolled away, and when my fist met fresh air, I collapsed in a fit of giggles, before relaxing on my back staring up into the flawless blue sky. We lay like that for quite a while, Daniel and I, side by side in companionable silence, until he stretched out his hand in an arc that encompassed the whole area.

"Don't you think that this is the most beautiful place in the entire world?"

His voice held a passion that echoed my own feelings, and I rose onto my elbow and picked a buttercup to hide the emotion that clogged my throat.

"Roll over onto your back," I urged, prodding him with my forefinger. He obliged with a broad grin, and I reached across to place the yellow flower beneath his chin.

"Now, let us see if you like butter."

When a yellow light shone on the tanned skin below his jaw, I laughed.

"There…you do."

For an instant our eyes met, and I had the strangest sense that I was drowning in those honey-brown depths. The scent of bluebells engulfed me. A roaring filled my ears, and, then suddenly, in one smooth movement, Daniel rolled me over onto my back and plucked a buttercup of his own.

"And do *you* like butter, Lucy McTavish?" he asked. When he placed the flower against my skin, time stood still.

His long lean body was suspended over mine, pinning me against the grass. Daniel…dear, comfortable, familiar Daniel was suddenly bringing out in me the strangest sensations.

"Do you, Lucy McTavish?" he asked again, his voice low and vibrant.

My eyes flickered toward his, whisper of a sigh escaped my lips, and although a strange lethargy had crept into my limbs, I somehow felt as if all my nerve endings were on fire. He felt it, too— I could see it in his warm brown eyes. And when he lowered his face to mine it seemed to me the most natural thing in the world.

None of the kisses I had ever experienced could even have begun to prepare me for the feel of Daniel's lips on mine. My entire body floated on a tide of ecstasy that shut out everything but his soft, warm mouth, and I knew that this was what I had been waiting for the whole of my life.

"Oh, Lucy." He pulled away to look into my eyes. "Why haven't we done this before?"

Holding his gaze, I gently touched his cheek, then I curled my fingers through the short thick hair at the base of his scull, overwhelmed by the longing to drown once again in the sensations flooded our bodies. And when his long tanned fingers crept across my tingling skin, I knew I could deny him nothing.

It was Daniel who drew away first.

"Should we be doing this, Luce?" he asked with a groan.

I lifted myself onto my elbow, just gazing at his larger-than-life features and lopsided grin. "Probably not," I told him with a smile.

While we brushed down our clothes, strangely awkward with each other, my eyes were drawn back again and again to Daniel, and every time I looked at him, he was looking at me. It felt as though we were all alone in our own little world, and I knew that there could be no going back to how things had been before.

We didn't say much on the way home, just rode together, acutely aware of each other's presence, yet still too unsure to voice our feelings. I wanted to talk to him, wanted to make sure that what had happened simply wasn't a dream, but some deep-rooted desire to hang on to our childhood stopped me. How could we ever be merely friends again after today?

And then we *were* back to how things had been, and a host of mundane jobs were calling for Daniel's attention. By the time I had seen to the horses, he had already gone to start the milking. On my way home, I peered around the barn door to say goodbye. The milking machine thumped rhythmically, and the warm, heavy aroma of cows rose up to meet me.

"See you, Lucy," called Mr. Brown.

"See you," I said, while my gaze sought out Daniel.

His eyes burned through the gloom in the far corner of the barn and his teeth flashed white.

"See you tomorrow, Luce," he murmured for my ears only, and I felt as though the world was opening up before me in a new, magical direction. For this was the start of the rest of my life...

★ ★ ★

Aunt V instantly knew what had happened. As soon as I walked through the door, my heart still singing, she looked into my eyes and she just knew.

"About time, too," she remarked with a grin.

"Time for what?" I queried, feeling the telltale flush creeping up my neck.

"Time that you two stopped playing games and got on with your lives."

"Is that what we've been doing?" I asked her. "Playing games?"

She shrugged, glancing across at my mother, and a frown flitted across her face.

"Perhaps that is what we all do."

The strangest thing happened then. As if a light had suddenly been switched on deep down somewhere inside her, my mother stood and walked toward me.

"I'm so happy for you Lucy," she cried, holding out her arms.

Nowadays, I could understand my mother's behavior much better. I knew that if she took her medication, she would be distant and strange, and if she didn't, she was likely to become agitated and overexcited, but this, this...awareness...was very different.

"Happy for what, Mom?" I asked, holding her slight body against mine.

"V says you're in love," she whispered against her fingers, like a child sharing a secret.

"And how would Aunt V know that?" I inquired.

"Are you?"

My aunt stood in front of the fireplace, shoulders back and arms straight down by her sides. Her stout, square figure was clad as always in sensible tweed, despite the heat, and I felt a warm rush of emotion for these two odd women who cared for me so much.

"Are you?" repeated Aunt V.

Was I? Was I in love? Is that what these strange feelings were all about? "How can you tell?" I asked her, and she smiled.

"Lucy," she told me, "I know you better than you know yourself, and you and that Daniel Brown have wasted enough years already."

All that night I tossed and tossed, going through the events of the day again, and again and every time I turned them around in my mind, they changed completely. When dawn's light crept at last through my window, I was no longer sure of anything. But the uncertainty was resolved the instant as I saw Daniel. At that moment, all my doubts were swept away as if they had never been. The touch of his hand, the sound of his voice, the sheer magnetism of his eyes—none of them had been a lie. His love for me was true, and mine for him was the most awesome emotion I had ever experienced.

After that weekend, that voyage of delicious discovery, there was no longer me and there was no longer Daniel; there was just "me and Daniel."

He phoned me and we talked for hours, but when I tried to recall our conversation, I couldn't remember a word we'd said. My every waking thought included him. My every dream was about him. My future and my past were his. If that was love, then yes, I was so deeply in love with Daniel Brown that without him I had no life. And if there are those who think that is sad, then I would say to them that they are the ones who are missing out.

★ ★ ★

It was in the meadow at Brookbank that we first made love. On a clear summer night, with the music of the tumbling stream in our ears, I reached an ecstasy that left me weeping in his arms. And after, when my eyes found his, I saw that he was crying, too.

"Oh, Lucy," he groaned, drawing me so closely against his hard-muscled chest that I could hear the heavy beating of his heart.

"Promise me that we'll always be together."

As I listened to the thumping of his life force, a strange fear washed over me and I clung to him.

"You promise," I urged. "Promise that you'll never leave me. No matter what happens you must promise."

His answer was to cover my lips with his. And then he drew back and ran his fingers tenderly across my brow.

"No matter what happens, I will never leave you, Lucy McTavish," he told me. "Remember that. No matter what happens, I will find a way to be with you."

Our wedding was arranged for the 25th of May, almost exactly one year from the day at Brookbank when we first discovered each other. Aunt V organized it with military precision, and even my mother seemed to have uncovered a whole new lease on life helping with the preparations. I found it scary sometimes that so many people should be dependent on our happiness. It all just seemed too good, somehow; too perfect to be true. I said as much one day to Mrs. Brown, who now insisted that I call her Edna.

"Lucy," she cried when I voiced my fears. "Don't you think you deserve some happiness?"

We were sitting in the kitchen at Homewood—the lovely kitchen that would soon be home to me.

"It just seems too good to be true," I reiterated. She laughed with delight and leaned across to give me a hug.

"And it seems too good to be true to me that you are going to be my daughter. But believe it, Lucy. It is true. Never be afraid of happiness."

I thought about what she said when I lay in my bed that night and I tried to chase away my fears. "Never be afraid of happiness," she had told me. "Take it while it's there and live for the moment."

But when the moment has gone, what then?

Daniel was standing in the yard at Homewood. The morning sunshine glinted on his hair, turning it to gold, and he lifted his hand to shade his eyes as he called to me.

"I'm off now, Luce, see you later. I'll pick you up at quarter to two." He grinned—that wide, lopsided grin that took over the whole of his face—and I ran across to kiss him goodbye.

"Don't forget to bring Promise in before you go," he reminded me.

I nodded, feeling the warmth of his cheek against my face as his lips touched mine.

"And don't you be late," I warned as he stepped onto his motorbike.

Daniel rarely rode his bike those days. It was one of the remnants of his teenage years, and he brought the bike out only occasionally on a sunny Sunday afternoon when the urge for speed overtook him. Today, though, he was working up the fell at Brookbank and he needed to leave early to come and meet me, so Bill, the elderly part-time farm help, was driving the pickup. It was already stacked with posts and wire and all the paraphernalia required to mend the fences. Bill started up its tired engine, and as it disappeared down the lane, Daniel revved his powerful motorbike.

"Don't be late," I reminded him yet again.

The heavy throbbing of the motor filled my ears. He rolled the bike forward, hand raised in farewell, and then he was gone, wheels spinning as he accelerated around the corner. A sense of panic rushed up my throat and an understanding hand closed around my arm.

"I wish he wouldn't drive so fast," remarked Edna Brown from behind me.

"You know Daniel," I responded with a worried smile.

"Never does anything slowly," she agreed, linking her arm through mine. As we walked together toward the kitchen door, my heart doubled its beat and I took a deep breath. Only a few hours and he would be back home safe

The sense of panic stayed with me as I mucked out the stables and saw to the horses, then took Daniel's dog, Buster, into the kitchen and said goodbye to Mrs. Brown, who was taking a steaming pie from the oven. Her round face was flushed with the heat and she flashed me a preoccupied smile.

"Don't be late for that estate agent," she reminded me.

"As if!" I retorted.

Today Daniel and I were going to see about renting a cottage just along the lane on the outskirts of the village. Our very first house together. As if either of us would be late for such an occasion. We had talked of little else since it had first come up a couple of weeks ago.

The trees stretched their motionless branches up into the clear blue sky and even the birds seemed to be resting in the warmth of the midday sun as my feet thudded along the deserted lane. Time felt suspended, and the panicky feeling that had lodged itself inside my throat made me reach for my mobile phone. I flicked down to Daniel's number, knowing that there was no signal beneath the sweep of the fell, at Brookbank. Sure enough, after two short rings my phone began an intermittent bleep. I stuffed the phone into my pocket and increased my speed, enjoying the effort that made my heart pound and my legs ache.

By one-thirty, I had showered and changed, and was eager to be off. I waited in the garden, sitting on the bench beside the front door, ears pricked for the throaty sound of a motorbike engine.

Aunt V had taken my mother into town to help her find a new hat to go with the lovely pale lilac suit she had bought for the wedding. I had never seen my mother so…normal. And Aunt V? Aunt V thought of nothing else. Sometimes I wished that Daniel and I had just run away and done it secretly because that was what our wedding was really all about, just me and Daniel and the rest of our lives, not cakes and hats and fancy outfits.

When he hadn't arrived by two o clock, the panic that had been with me all morning swelled into a horrible foreboding. I tried to shake it off, but my breath came in short gasps and my heart fluttered inside my chest. Something was wrong; I knew it. I dialed his number again and again, but all I got was a distant, curt voice: *The person you are calling is unavailable. Please try later.* How much later, and where was Daniel? I tried Homewood, but the phone rang on and on. What was happening? Where was Edna Brown?

At two-thirty I started to run along the lane, back toward the farm, all thoughts of our cottage forgotten as I cried out for Daniel.

The battered white pickup was in the yard, abandoned outside the rear door, and old Bill Armitage stood, cap in hand, staring at the ground, his face distorted by worry as he spoke to Daniel's dad. My heart closed up as I ran toward them.

"I don't know where he is," he was saying. "He left early, soon after twelve. I told him he had plenty of time... Then I saw his motorbike in the back of a tow truck—or at least, it looked like Daniel's bike."

"Then where is he?"

My voice felt as though it came from someone else. It sounded hollow in my ears, hollow and distant and slightly distorted. I felt though I *was* someone else. This couldn't be happening to Lucy McTavish.

"Where's Daniel?" I screamed.

"I'm ringing the hospital," announced Edna Brown. She was standing in the kitchen doorway, face pale fingers twisted into her apron.

"I'll insist that they tell me if there has been anyone admitted."

"Now, don't jump to conclusions, Edna."

Mr. Brown, always levelheaded, placed a hand on his wife's arm.

"Chances are his bike just broke down and Bill saw the garage picking it up."

"Then why didn't he ring us?" snapped Mrs. Brown. With wooden legs, I followed her into the house, knowing it was hopeless, knowing it was over. But he had promised not to leave me that day at Brookbank a lifetime ago.

Remember that. No matter what happens, I will find a way to be with you. I could see his dear face in front of me now as he'd made that promise, the first time we'd loved each other. I clung fiercely to the memory. Whatever had happened, he *would* keep that promise. I knew it with no shadow of a doubt.

Mrs. Brown stood in the hallway, bristling with all the

indignation she could muster, channeling her fear into anger as she held the phone against her ear.

"Well, you may as well tell me," she insisted, "because I'm on my way to the hospital now. I know you had a young man admitted from a motorbike accident this afternoon, and I want to know how he is."

There was an empty silence then, a sudden chilling silence.

"It was what...?" she whispered.

The phone slipped from her shaking fingers to clatter onto the ground, and the clatter echoed and echoed inside my head, mingling with a high-pitched distant scream as the floor came up to meet me.

London, England
Months later

From the moment I awoke I just knew today was...different, although I didn't yet know why. I climbed out of bed, and my bare feet cringed at the coolness of the gleaming wood floor, before they plunged ecstatically into the warm softness of a thick cream rug. In the bathroom, the sound of tap water filled my head like a waterfall crashing onto rocks, and when I looked at the sky through the bathroom window, it was so clear that I paused, toothbrush aloft, to stare with a kind of awe at the tiny white cloud drifting across the ocean of blue.

Hidden memories rushed in, unbidden. Memories of another, wider sky, a sky that seemed to stretch into eternity. Uncomfortable with my new awareness, unwilling to face the festering pain that the memories provoked, I closed my eyes, concentrating on the feel of the toothbrush against my teeth.

Alex's deep voice brought me sharply back to the present. "I'll be late tonight."

I glanced round self-consciously to meet his brooding gaze, the same penetrating gaze that had drawn me to him all those months ago.

I didn't think that there would ever be anyone else after Daniel, but Alex was just so compelling. His fierce dark eyes had locked on me from across the dance floor of the dingy club that Nicola had eventually succeeded in dragging me to. Every time I looked up, he was there, his expression impenetrable from behind those hypnotic eyes. And before the night was over, he had somehow prized my phone number from behind my painstakingly built defenses.

All that felt like a lifetime ago now, but still I stopped sometimes to wonder how he had managed to get past Daniel. For Danny Brown was the love of my life, and Alex was... Alex was just Alex.

He stood behind me now, confident and sure. Navy suit, pale blue shirt, dark blue understated silk tie, immaculate as always.

"Okay," I murmured.

Nodding briefly, he pivoted on his heel; then his shoes tapped along the hallway and down the wooden staircase. The front door slamming reverberated inside my head, and I clutched my arms around myself, stifling the shiver inside me. For today felt different, although I didn't yet know why.

Realizing that I was going to be late for work, I dashed into the bedroom and flung open the wardrobe. Late or not, today I needed something bright and fresh to wear, something that would make a statement.

Black clothes hung in front of me, neatly arranged in utterly straight rows. The scent of expensive perfume floated into my nostrils. I felt as though someone else's life paraded before me. But it wasn't someone else's, was it? It was mine.

Long-contained emotion flooded me, and I shut my eyes tightly, clinging to the image of Alex's fierce black eyes, fighting off the memories I had forbidden my self for so long. This *was* my life now. These expensive, elegant garments belonged to me. Yet they didn't really. Like everything else in this perfect house, they belonged to Alex. Did that include me? Did I belong to Alex, too?

Frantically I began to rummage through the clothes, rebellion swelling as I searched for a glimpse of... And suddenly there it was, a flash of crimson at the end of the rack, resplendent against the ocean of black. Reverently I withdrew the vivid red suit, quivering as I lovingly stroked the material. I threw back my shoulders and held the suit high, reveling in newfound delight. It was perfect for today— I just knew it. Somewhere there were shoes to match. I remembered them vaguely, high-heeled and strappy, totally *unsuitable* for a day at the office, but totally suitable for me.

When I was ready, I preened in front of the mirror, imagining Alex's expression were he to see me now. He hated red—or any other bright color come to that— preferring me to wear nothing but black. "Having class," he'd called it while shaking his head at my casual jeans and nice big "lazy day" sweater. And eventually, I suppose, he had gotten his way, for I couldn't recall the last time I'd dressed in anything casual. Today, though... Today was for me.

I ran my fingers through my hair, allowing it to fluff into a cloud around my pale, heart-shaped face and stared critically at the image in front of me. I liked my hair. I hated my wide mouth and I thought my gray eyes were much too far apart, but I loved my long, dark, wavy hair. Alex liked me to have it pinned neatly on top of my head.

I closed my eyes, conjuring his handsome face. I was being disloyal. Alex had taught me to live again, when I had felt my life to be over. I owed him for that.

For an instant, a picture of Daniel's happy-go-lucky, irregular features jumped into my mind. I pushed it away before the pain forced itself back from where it was locked deep in my heart and turned abruptly from the mirror.

Outside, I walked along the pavement in a daze, taking in the sights and sounds of another busy weekday morning as if they were all new to me, savoring the bustling urgency of lives that never last. It had rained in the night, and the streets were a glistening gray, setting off the figures of people scurrying to work, heads low despite the colorful garments they wore to fend off the rain. Only the children's faces lit up the morning. They wandered by in giggling groups, eyes shining with laughter, expressions mirroring the intensity I felt but could not understand. Some hugged their homework to their chests and chattered excitedly as they ran for the bus. Others threw their bags up into the air, loitering to sneak a cigarette behind the huge sycamore tree near the bus stop.

My bus was already waiting when I arrived at the stop. I hesitated, watching the line diminish as the waiting people poured through the bus door like sheep, knowing no better than to follow one another on the dreary road of routine.

But I had a choice. I lifted my chin, relishing the fresh breeze against my face, and carried on walking.

I took the shortcut across the park, where oak and ash and

sycamore reached their branches way up into the graying sky, bringing a hint of the countryside into the city. I paused for a moment, staring at their huge majestic shapes as a gust of wind brought autumn leaves fluttering down. They twirled around my head before, settling gently on the ground to form a carpet of red and gold and glorious flame especially for me. With a smile in my heart I started to run, sliding through the leaves in my silly red shoes. Tripping over a tree stump and almost falling on my face in the thick, wet leaves.

"Are you all right?"

I didn't notice the man approaching at a jog from along the other pathway until he spoke. He was thirty something, tall and broad, his dark hair short and tousled. His honey-brown eyes sparkled with an amused glint as he slowed to a walk, then stopped in front of me. He leaned forward, hands pressed against the tanned muscles of his thighs, his pleasant face flushed with effort.

"Are you running away from something?" he asked.

His voice was deep, with the slightest Scottish burr.

I slithered upright and returned to the everyday world, my face as crimson as my suit.

"No…no…thank you. I'm just—"

"Enjoying the morning?" he said for me.

I couldn't help but smile. "Something like that."

"Not the best footwear to go for a run in," he commented.

"They match my suit," I offered lamely, glancing down at my damp feet.

He laughed, a great bellow that echoed in the treetops.

"And a very nice suit it is, too," he remarked, his eyebrows raised in appreciation.

"Aren't you supposed to be running?" I ventured.

He shrugged, pulling a face. "Well, as I'm not actually running anywhere in particular, I don't suppose it matters."

"Ah." I smiled. "I see. You must be one of those sad fitness freaks who get up at the crack of dawn to put in fifteen miles before breakfast."

For a moment he caught my eyes again, and something stirred inside me, some distant memory of that exact expression.

"Have we met before?"

We said it in unison, then giggled like two old friends.

"Seriously, though…" he began.

"Have we met before?" I finished for him.

He smiled at me and I smiled back, mesmerized by the golden glints in his brown eyes. A peculiar warmth spread through my body, right to the ends of my fingertips.

"We can't have," he told me. "Because I would definitely have remembered."

An awkward moment followed, and then I set off again along the pathway. What was I doing anyway, talking to strangers in the park?

"Decided not to run anymore?" he inquired, falling into step beside me.

I walked sedately toward the busy hum of the city to reenter my life, focusing on the snowy carpet beneath my feet and trying to ignore him.

"You know you shouldn't really talk to strangers in parks," he told me, uncannily echoing my thoughts as we approached the gates.

Ahead of us I could see the traffic flowing by, heard angry horns honking with impatience. I hesitated, taking in the moment, my whole body bursting with awareness.

"Today is special, though," I said.

"How? How is it special?"

His eyes mine like those of a friend, and I was acutely reminded yet again of Daniel Brown. After months of keeping his memory at bay, today for some reason he was flooding my soul.

"I just feel…"

There in the gateway to the park, suspended between the glowing autumn beauty of the woodland and the harsh gray concrete of the city, I stared at the familiar stranger, wanting to share my odd, explosive emotions. But there are no words to explain what you don't understand.

"Special," I told him. "Today everything *feels* special."

"Well, I hope it will always stay special for you," he murmured, touching my cheek in a gesture of farewell. And then he just turned and walked away from me, back toward the park, while I stood alone and confused in the busy street as the town hall clock began to chime.

★ ★ ★ ★ ★

Lucy McTavish has found the love of her life—
but what happens when she loses him? Daniel Brown
broke his promise to be with her forever. Or did he?
A Heartbeat Away is a different kind of romance, a story
about a love so powerful it restores hope…and life.

A Heartbeat Away is on sale February 27 for a limited
time from Harlequin® Everlasting Love™.

Look for savings on the next page.

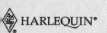

® HARLEQUIN®

E V E R L A S T I N G   L O V E™

Every great love has a story to tell™

Available wherever books are sold, including most bookstores, supermarkets, drugstores and discount stores.

Receive $1.⁰⁰ off

A HEARTBEAT AWAY
or any other Harlequin®
Everlasting Love™ title.

Coupon expires June 30, 2007.
Redeemable at participating
retail outlets in the U.S. only.
Limit one coupon per customer.

113938

5 65373 00076 2   (8100) 0 11393

AHACOUPUS

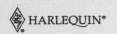

HARLEQUIN®

EVERLASTING LOVE™

Every great love has a story to tell™

*Available wherever books are sold, including most
bookstores, supermarkets, drugstores and discount stores.*

Receive $1.⁰⁰ off

A HEARTBEAT AWAY
or any other Harlequin®
Everlasting Love™ title.

Coupon expires June 30, 2007.
Redeemable at participating
retail outlets in Canada only.
Limit one coupon per customer.

CANADIAN RETAILERS: Harlequin Enterprises Limited will pay the face value of
this coupon plus 10.25¢ if submitted by the customer for this specified product only.
Any other use constitutes fraud. Coupon is nonassignable. Void if taxed, prohibited
or restricted by law. Void if copied. Consumer must pay for any government taxes.
Nielson Clearing House customers ("NCH") submit coupons and proof of sales
to: Harlequin Enterprises Ltd., P.O. Box 3000, Saint John, N.B. E2L 4L3. Non–NCH
retailer—for reimbursement submit coupons and proof of sales directly to Harlequin
Enterprises Ltd., Retail Marketing Department, 225 Duncan Mill Rd., Don Mills,
Ontario M3B 3K9, Canada. Limit one coupon per customer. Valid in Canada only.

52607716

AHACOUPCAN

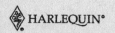